I0618824

DEVON
PRIDEAUX
GHOST
STORIES

FEATURING THE PRIDIAS FAMILY OF

DEVON

13TH - 16TH CENTURY

A CIP catalogue record for this title is

available from the British Library.

ISBN 978-0-9954609-7-3

www.paganuspublishing.co.uk

First Published in 2017

Paganus Publishing

Ruthin

Denbighshire

Paganus Publishing

FOREWORD

Devon Prideaux Ghost Stories is one of the books in the series of the Pridias/Prideaux family throughout the centuries. Other titles are **Cornish Prideaux Ghost Stories, Collected Prideaux Ghost Stories, A Ghost Story, A Christmas Story, More Prideaux Ghost Stories, Further Prideaux Ghost Stories** and **Prideaux Ghost Stories**.

The Sheriff of Devon features Roger de Pridias, and the story introduces the Mothecombe Coven where his wife is a senior member. A talisman owned by Edmund, Earl of Cornwall is brought to the temple in Mothecombe woods for verification.

The Mothecombe Coven features Peter de Pridias and his rediscovery of the book written by his Cornish ancestor Richard de Pridias. He discovers how powerful and influential his parents are in the County and the coven.

Ice Day at Sequers Bridge features Sir Roger de Pridias. His story is about an very unusual occurrence with a huge flying metal carriage which abducts Sir Roger and some other locals during the coldest Winter on record.

Big, Black Rats features Sir John de Pridias and his family and the battle they had with the large rats which roam the lands and begin to attack people and animals.

Ghost Ship features Giles Prideaux and his meetings with Geoffrey Chaucer and John Hawley at Dartmouth where they discuss the recent ghost ship sightings.

Burial Ground features Sir John Prideaux and his visit to an ancient copse on his land. There he is forced to see the ghosts from his past.

It is difficult to recognise a ghost features William Prideaux and his jealousy of his wife's relationship with their friend William Woolacombe and its tragic outcome.

The Terror of the Thunderstorm features John Prideaux and the unusual and terrible storms which are frightening the residents and killing some of them.

CONTENTS

THE SHERIFF OF DEVON

Featuring Roger de Pridias (1224 - 1291)

It's one thing to know that children are involved in coven meetings, but quite another to do something about it.

Roger was serving his third year as High Sheriff of Devon, a role given to him originally by Richard, Earl of Cornwall because of his close friendship and trust in Roger. His service in that role continued following Richard's death which had been caused by grief following the murder of his son Henry, by the de Montforts.

Roger was good friends with Edmund, Richard's second son who was to inherit titles previously destined for Henry, one of which was 2nd Earl of Cornwall. Edmund continued his associations with the Pridias family both in Cornwall and Devon after his father's death, even though the family had always been more friends with Richard than Edmund.

Edmund was often in London as he pursued his goals, but travelled back to the South West, mainly by ship. He docked at Orcherton, Ponts Mill or Helston and other small ports, dependent upon his aims at the time. He spent much of his time at Restormel, a little north of Pridias Hall and regularly went to Trematon and Tintagel, both being castles that he loved. **Edmund's father** Richard, the King of Almain and first Earl of Cornwall, had acquired these properties during his lifetime. He had successfully persuaded Gervase de Hornicote to exchange Tintagel Castle for some manors around Haylesford. Richard in 1236, then added the curtain wall and the great ward on the mainland which was linked to the island by a bridge. This move was to help ingratiate himself with the Cornish by affirming and accepting the Cornish link with King Arthur as had been written by Geoffrey of Monmouth. Richard also obtained Restormel and all lands on the east of the road between Bodmin and Lostwithiel from the heiress, Isolda de Cardinham.

Edmund loved Restormel so much that he made **Lostwithiel** the capital of his county. It became his seat of government where tinners came with their blocks of metal and was the site of the goal where many transgressors suffered the ultimate penalty of hanging. Edmund however would not help the poverty stricken and already tumbledown Tywardreath Priory. Instead he relied on the hermits who were spiritual descendants of the early saints, for his own spiritual progress.

The Cornish branch of the Pridias family had been party to and witnesses of, these contracts. They had their feet firmly under the table.

The Knights of Cornwall and Devon disliked Edmund, mistrusted him and resented him. Many would have

preferred Henry, but he was dead and his murderers punished with only excommunication. Roger, perceived by many to being in league with Edmund, was not popular among his neighbours. He was unfazed because the affiliation was making him richer by the day. He had even offered to buy back the Pridias lands in Cornwall, but had his offer refused even though his kin were in dire need of financial injection.

Roger sat many times in the Shire courts and unable to be swayed by bribes, often ruled against his own countrymen. He raised more tax for the Crown than was considered acceptable locally and he made many enemies. He considered himself to be a fair man, believing in the rights of all men and women. He played a great part in helping in establishing the borough of **Modbury** which now had a weekly market and two annual fairs. Roger also encouraged development by granting charters to peasants who were able to extend their holdings field by field as they colonised waste land. He wanted each man to have the opportunity to better himself. But he had many arguments and litigation battles and it began to wear him down.

His parents Geoffrey and Isabella, had given him a great deal of land on his marriage to Gilda, a kinswoman of the Reskymer family of Haylesford. Roger had only to pay for this privilege with one pair of white gloves or one penny if he found it impossible to find the white gloves, to Isabella. Roger also took control of land and property around Haylesford, which had been bequeathed to his wife.

They not only ensured that all their children were born at Haylesford, but conceived in Cornwall.

Roger and Gilda considered themselves Cornish and not Devonian. Geoffrey had told Roger that he and his brother were conceived and born in Cornwall too and Roger hoped to persuade his own children to consider themselves Cornishmen who owned owning Devon lands, rather than the other way about.

Edmund cared not about Cornishmen and their urge to remain as such, but he did care about the magical abilities of some people and knew quite well of the Melusine blood which flowed through their veins. It was said that the golden-haired Gilda was of this blood and this fact had encouraged Roger to marry her, upon Richard the first Earl of Cornwall's, recommendation. Gilda for her part knew of her bloodline but had no conscious knowledge of her abilities and Roger hoped that these would rise to the surface before long.

He knew that it was only a matter of time before he would be dismissed from his role and felt that he wanted it to be on his own terms and no one else's. Gilda and her friends could help him in this goal. Roger had begun to make plans in that regard but Edmund again stood in his way.

Edmund had obtained several items and relics said to be connected to Jesus. In a pendant reminiscent of the one once owned by Charlemagne, Edmund had a blood relic of Jesus which he had purloined on his Crusading skirmishes. He had been envious of

Charlemagne's talisman and so had a jeweller envelop his own relic with gold and jewels. Edmund had shown it to Roger and Gilda and they had agreed with him that they should use the skills of the Mothecombe coven in order to establish its authenticity.

Edmund was ecstatic with the suggestion and promised Roger that he would let him have another of his minor relics in return for this service. A few shreds of the shroud fashioned into a ring which could be worn on a man's little finger, he said. Roger remembered the conversation he had the previous night with Gilda.

"That cross and shroud must have been massive, the number of relics that have come from them. And the blood of Jesus? Enough to fill a lake."

Roger had laughed with his wife but he had no intention of laughing with Edmund. He was notoriously emotionally unpredictable and Roger lived on a knife edge during each conversation with him. They had agreed to have him meet the coven because to refuse would have meant consequences. Gilda was a member and while they helped some women find partners or get pregnant, they also helped men with their business dealings and political ambitions. This coven was accepted in the locality and consulted by many. Their identities were secret in order to prevent repercussions and this was facilitated by the gowns and hoods they wore.

They weren't that harmless though. Gilda had read the documents that her father-in-law had left and had understood their meaning, suddenly, on the thirtieth reading. She now knew how life worked and how it was not only possible, but necessary that any person living could control their own life and the lives of others.

Did she have Melusine blood? Her family said so and Roger hoped so. Whenever she returned home to Helford to give birth, the old women and maids who attended her births confirmed that the new baby did what all Melusine children did – they opened their eyes as soon as they took their first breath. None of her babies behaved like a vulnerable creature, but as a small adult awaiting its maturity.

Gilda now considered her family complete with Piers, Reginald, Thomas, Alice and Lucy. Roger agreed and accepted her instructions that he must no longer bother her in that regard and that he was quite welcome to take a mistress. Roger didn't, preferring to remain true to Gilda and he was also finding that he was constantly stressed about his knife-edge friendship with Edmund.

The night that Edmund was allowed to enter the coven interior was kept secret from all but coven members and Edmund's personal guards. Edmund had been sworn to secrecy and had been told and believed that the witches would be able to tell if he had told about the meeting.

The coven met in the copious woods at Mothecombe which spread along the coastline and the estuary sides inland to Ermington and beyond. These woods were matched in their density and confusion on the opposite side of the banks of the River Erme. It was said that only the witches could find the stone archway which marked their own chapel. Others had tried and failed and worse, had become hopelessly lost in the process. Seekers ended up on the beaches beneath the banks at low tide, hailing passing boats and begging for rescue.

Edmund arrived on horseback to the edge of the woodland and was met by twenty hooded and cloaked beings. It was impossible to tell whether they were male or female and he shivered with excitement. His guards had their hands on the sword hilts, ready to draw them at a moment's notice, but Edmund told them to desist. Roger clapped his hands and asked that they all leave their horses where they were and his men would take care of them.

The gold-robed figures turned in unison and moved into the darkness of the woods. Although it was a darkly cloudy night the glimmer of the moon reflected off the cloaks, seemingly lighting the way. Roger was excited, he loved these nights. He was proud of his wife and her abilities and the results she obtained from her practices. Edmund and his men would not know that she was the figure with the silver Celtic cross embroidered on the back of her cloak which would only become visible when lighted at certain angles by moon, lamp or fire.

One figure lightly beat a skin drum in time to their steps and no words were spoken. They moved deeper and deeper into the darkness and even Roger, accustomed as he was to the ceremony, felt himself jump when strange noises echoed through the trees.

It was 30 minutes before the group arrived at the stone archway and the drumming stopped.

Edmund asked, "Is this it Roger? Are we here?"

"Ssssh Sir," instructed one of the figures and Edmund obeyed.

There was a glow from the chapel window and the group moved towards it and entered one by one. Roger indicated the way to Edmund who clutched his talisman to his breast as he entered the room. The door was closed behind him and Roger pointed out the wall hangings of heavy blue cloth, woven with threads of gold, silver and many other colours, depicting scenes of sorcery. Or this was how it appeared to Edmund when he saw the enchanted creatures and the wise men and women standing by monuments. At the far end was a large oak table upon which sat items of gold and silver and where candles and incense burned. A small man was attending to the table and its contents. He checked and rechecked the order in which the items were set out and Edmund wondered why that was so important.

In front of the table were three thrones, the middle throne larger than the other two and three robed figures sat upon them. This was a signal to the other figures who sat on the benches lining the walls. Roger beckoned Edmund to walk through the centre of the group and had him place his talisman on the table on a blue silken cloth. This, Roger neatly arranged and then covered it with another piece of blue silk. Edmund looked alarmed at its apparent disappearance but Roger raised his hand in demonstration of there being no need to worry. Edmund was allocated a covered seat in the corner of the chapel between the head three and the rest of the coven.

Roger sat in another corner and watched as the coven stood before moving towards the centre of the room and then turning to face the still seated three. They bowed in unison and the three dipped their heads in acknowledgement. The small man lifted the gold plate containing the silk and the talisman and brought it to the throned three and dropped to his knees while offering the plate to them. The centre figure took the plate from him and placed it on the wide arm of his own throne. Roger glanced across at Edmund to see if he was upset about the process, him being a minor part of it, but Edmund seemed perfectly happy and focussed.

The middle figure stood and raised the covered plate to the ceiling, which Edmund had only just realised was painted as a night sky with stars, planets and chariots carrying God-like men and women. As the figure chanted in unison with the group, one of the painted figures leaned down from his place in the ceiling painting and turned into a coloured mist as he fell to the ground. He reformed as a life-sized man dressed in Biblical robes and soon he was joined by his counterparts from the ceiling.

Roger never ceased to be amazed by this and noticed that Edmund had his mouth wide open and his eyes goggled as he turned to Roger. Roger put his finger to his lips and smiled at his Royal superior and Edmund obeyed by snapping his mouth shut and returning his gaze to the strange scene.

The spirits, for they must have been spirits, clicked their fingers and another line of hooded figures entered the chapel. Roger had never seen these before and from their movement and their high-pitched whimpering, it was clear that these were children. He couldn't stop himself saying,

"What is this? Why are there children here? Who ordered this?"

His answer came in the form of a sharp thump in his back and his arms were pulled behind him.

"Silence now, Sir Roger. We must all do as we are told within these walls."

"I most certainly do not," Roger answered. "This is my chapel and my ceremony. You cannot frighten me."

"You should be frightened Sir. They seem impressed with this talisman you have brought us."

The grip grew tighter and Roger stifled the cry he felt, for he had no idea who this robed coven member was, nor could he identify his own wife amongst the others. This meeting was different to before and he knew not why. He was dragged roughly back to the wall and tied to a chair.

The spirits took the talisman from the platter and the first spirit put it around his neck. Roger could not see how Edmund was taking this, but he could hear no complaints. The robed figures began to move in a clockwise direction around the centre group, who knelt at the feet of the talisman wearer as he turned his face and hands to the ceiling and began a chant. This was taken up by the rest and as the noise became a vibration, the walls of the chapel disappeared and the painted sky and stars became part of the experience. The trees in the woods were faintly visible in the background with no chapel walls between. And all were now standing, then dancing in mid-air, with stars and planets surrounding them.

Roger had seen similar before but he was still worried. This experience was stronger and it felt as though they were the visitors in an unknown place instead of visitor Gods granting their silly questions and requests. And the children, that had never happened.

The children had already been ushered to the centre and the talisman-wearing God instructed that they surround him in a tight group. The children were crying now, no longer whimpering.

Roger said, "You cannot harm them! Leave the children!"

The children were frightened even further by this shout and some were trying to run away. There was no door and so their struggles were met by laughs and grabs before they were returned to the talisman God. After ten minutes of this fruitless effort, the children began to quieten and stay where they had been put.

The talisman-God raised his arms aloft and Roger saw that he now carried a glittering sword. As Roger shouted, "No!" the sword was brought to the God's waist and he span around quickly, mowing down each child as he did so.

When Roger woke, he found Gilda sitting next to him, cradling his head in her hands.

"Roger! My dear Roger! Are you alright? You were so strange tonight."

"The children. What about the children?"

"Our children? They are at home or at their own homes."

"I mean tonight's children. The ones that were killed."

"Killed? No one was killed. Why would children be killed here?"

Gilda was genuinely concerned and beckoned to another to help her with her husband.

Edmund had enjoyed himself, Roger was told. He had received confirmation that his talisman was genuine and could bring him nothing but good luck and so had ridden away to Restormel with his guards. He had expressed his thanks to Gilda and asked that she inform the seemingly unwell Roger that his assistance would be rewarded. He had handed her an ornate ring and Gilda promised to give it to her husband when he recovered. This she now did and placed it on Roger's little finger.

Roger sat up and saw that he was lying between the archway and the chapel. The coven members had all but gone, leaving only Gilda, the small man and William Abbott, his own man.

"I need to go back inside the chapel," said Roger.

"Why my love? Let us go home now. Everything has been cleaned up and you know as well as I do that to return will mean that I have to go through the whole process of cleansing again."

Roger did know this to be true for it was the spells that protected the area and kept it from prying eyes. Gilda would not want her work undone, she was tired enough.

"We all did well tonight, Roger," she said to him. "Edmund will make sure that we never want for money or assistance and he will consider himself in your debt."

"You cast that one too then?"

"Of course, I did. Times are too difficult not to have influential friends in very high places."

"And there was me thinking that it was my political skill and good company which kept him close."

"Don't be ridiculous Roger," she said.

"Fetch my horse my dear, while I go behind a tree."

She laughed and walked away from him as he struggled to his feet. Roger felt ill and dizzy and that worried him as he had never been this way at any other meeting. As he watered the tree he thought about what generally happened and this time, apart from Edmund being present it had only been the children that was different. Yet everyone else denied their presence there and yet he had seen them killed! Had he though? Had he been bewitched by the others?

Gilda was riding back to him and leading his horse. The servants had fetched them from the edge of the wood as they would now be able to navigate the trees without assistance. Mothecombe woods had changed again.

"Here you are my love," she said as she threw him the reins.

"I saw the children," he insisted.

"There are no dead children here Roger. Look around you."

He did and could see nothing.

"You were happy with the talisman?"

"Oh, yes we were. It seems a shame that a stupid man such as Edmund should have ownership of such an important and powerful item."

"It has power?"

"It has a great deal of power Roger and I don't believe that Edmund is a fit man to have it."

"But he has it nevertheless."

"So it would appear."

And that was still his problem. He knew, he just knew that children had been there and if that were so, they must have been killed. Or perhaps they had been sent to another dimension, many existed he was fully aware of that. He knew that death did not happen as almost everyone believed it would. We are all dead already and choose how to spend our long journey while we wait to wake up. That was the essence of the teachings Richard had left the family. To understand it was to believe it and to use all day, every day and yet these words, written in plain sight were unbelievable to most and therefore useless.

Following this night, Edmund had kept to his word and helped Roger's appointments and his career and Gilda had become head of the Mothecombe coven and was powerful. Roger was benefiting in her wake. Property deals and land acquisition were already falling into his lap. And he liked it.

Roger had just had a meeting with three local women, famous for their do-gooding about the neighbourhood and they had told him that an alarming number of children had been going missing recently.

"Granted my Lord, they are the children of vagabonds and thieves and dirty gypsies. But it does not mean that they should be stolen."

"I have heard tell that witches and devil worshippers want children because it furthers their powers," said her friend.

"I doubt that is true," answered Roger.

"Well perhaps you don't see what goes on, hidden here in your big house, Sir Roger. But I am telling you something funny is happening."

"Do you have any idea of who may be involved?"

"No, my Lord. Shall I let you know if I find anything out?"

"Indeed yes. I should be most interested. In fact, you must inform me and no one else."

"Of course, my Lord." She bobbed a curtsey and they all left, happy that his Lordship would be taking care of the matter.

Any notion of following up on these thoughts was reduced sharply when he immediately received notice from his estate manager that Roger was now the new owner of some more Devon property.

The spells were working.

When they were undressing that night, Gilda had her jewellery chest open as she returned her ruby necklace to its container. Roger recognised a glint from another half-opened box and when Gilda left the room to visit her washroom, he looked inside.

It was the talisman.

If not it, then a jolly good replica of it. He picked it up and held it and knew that it was the original. He returned it swiftly and ran to his side of the bed before Gilda saw him.

"Gilda. That talisman of Edmund's. How powerful would it be if we had possession of it?"

"And a replica had been returned to Edmund during all the smoke and mirrors confusion, you mean?"

"Well, yes."

"We would be the most powerful family in the South West. In the country. Why do you ask?"

"No reason, my dear. Just curious."

He got into bed as Gilda snapped the chest shut and locked it.

THE MOTHECOMBE COVEN

Featuring Peter de Pridias (1260-1316)

Now that his father was dead, Peter felt that he had to get to the bottom of the conundrum. For it was surely that, in this year of 1299.

During the summer, Peter's father Roger had settled some of his Cornish property on Peter and if Peter were to die without heirs, then the inheritance would pass to his younger brother Reginald and if he died, the properties were to go to his then single daughter Marjery and her heirs before it would go to his other two daughters and their husbands. Roger had not known at his death that Marjery was being pursued by Richard Heligan and he would have heartily approved of their subsequent marriage and children. Perhaps she told him all about it when she died during the birth of her second child only a few years later.

Roger had wanted to ensure that his other son Thomas would be so far away from the money and properties that he and his family would never inherit. Roger would be receiving a fair income for this until he died and at that time his Devon and other Cornish properties were bequeathed in the same way.

Peter was given in trust, Brodoke and Redwall and the lands, woods, manor and tenements for a fee payable each Easter and in its entirety following his parents' deaths. These vast swathes of Cornwall were as dear to Peter as they had been to Roger and Geoffrey and he determined to keep them in his family in addition to the Devon properties. In some ways, the Cornish properties were dearer to him - he was still a strong blood Cornishman. It was understood that there would be nothing for Thomas, not upon his marriage to Isolda and not upon the death of his father.

Thomas had been told and told not to marry her. Isolda was the daughter of one of the coven members and she and Gilda did not get on. Isolda's mother Anastasia, was aiming for a better position within the membership and had tried some spells of her own to gain her wish. But she was a weakling, a junior compared to Gilda and all she achieved was Gilda's wrath and a binding spell. Thomas's marriage was forbidden, but he went ahead anyway and banished himself from his own family. No one sent him good wishes on the birth of his son whom he had named Roger, after his father.

His second brother Reginald, had been going to marry a wonderful Cornish girl called Marjery Chartery, a Prideaux cousin via her mother and yet another rumoured Melusine descendant. She was tiny and red haired and hailed from Luxulyan. Reginald had met her on one of his trips to Pridias with his father and Peter. They were making a visit to their lands and houses at Bradoc and their manor on the banks of the river opposite Golant. Roger had inherited these lands from Geoffrey along with several Cornish properties at Rodewell. When Reginald saw her standing on the riverbank that day, her hair blowing in the wind, he fell in love right there and then.

The whole family were ecstatic and Gilda took Marjery to her coven meetings which she seemed to enjoy. Then, two days before the wedding to Reginald, Marjery was found dead on the same river bank he first saw her. after having been lured from her house in the middle of the night. Reginald was inconsolable and despite his mother's begging, he joined the priesthood. Roger ensured that Reginald became the Rector of Bradoc in their Cornish manor so that he would always be near his beloved Marjery who was buried in the churchyard there. Reginald paid for a stone representation of her, arms folded aloft her tomb and spent as much time there as he could. Reginald gave his own lands and inheritance to Peter when he became a priest.

His sisters had married well, having better luck than two of their brothers. Alice married Richard Reskymer, a landowner and businessman of Helston, and Lucy married Benedict Reynward, a fabulously wealthy landowner and tin mine owner from Cornwall. His family had interests in Liskeard, St Minver, Bodmin and many more towns. Their youngest sister Marjery married Richard Heligan, another landed Cornishman who was to inherit the lands near Mevagissey.

They all helped each other out, unless business interests clashed and that happened more often than not. But blood was blood and it usually came out alright in the end. There were no long-term arguments and that was why no one had been really surprised when Roger announced that there had been a change in his mind and he now wanted to leave money and a manor to his previously estranged son, Thomas. He said that he wanted to bring him back into the family and included his children in that bequest. Peter's wife Clarice, mentioned that perhaps it was easier for Roger to do such a thing now that Isolda was so pious and determined to ingratiate herself back into the Pridias fold. Also, she had heard that they were running short of money.

Peter had agreed that some of the properties which had been previously going to Reginald, now firmly ensconced in his religious life, could pass to Thomas and his heirs. The deed was done on the 29th September 1291, two weeks prior to Roger's death and Roger was happy that he could leave his properties in good hands. Clarice told Peter that Isolda was positively wagging her tail with excitement and had quickly begun trying to get nominated to the Mothecombe coven. Three members must nominate her for her application to be considered. Then, four weeks after his father's death, Thomas insisted that his inheritance be returned to Peter and that he wanted nothing more to do with it.

"But your son and his children? They must have something to live on after you have gone? Lord knows you have little enough as it is!"

"We have the manor from Isolda and I have been told that there will be enough income from the farms and orchards."

"It isn't much Thomas. I have so much here and in Cornwall and now that Reginald is a God follower and all the girls gone to their husbands, I want you to share it with me."

Even Peter was surprised at how emotional he felt about it. Perhaps it was that only a few years ago, they had been six children playing and riding together. Often, they would be brought on display as beautifully well-dressed specimens at parties that their parents hosted. But, more often than not they were in the care of maids and teachers. Peter would remember the fun the siblings had had in so many beautiful houses of their own, or belonging to close family in both Devon and Cornwall. Drummed into their minds was the information that they were a Cornish family with rich Cornish blood and told that they must in the future marry only Cornish men and women and ensure that their children were born in Cornwall. They had all done as they were told, believing strongly in the Pridias line. All except Thomas. He had married the Devon woman who, although of good blood, was not of good Cornish blood.

"My son will never survive his illness and there will no line stretching on from my blood Peter. I don't want the lands to leave too. If I die before Isolda, she will leave it to her ridiculous nephews. You have it back, Isolda will go mental when she finds out but I really don't care about that. She has her affairs while I…"

"You are not happy, are you brother? I wish you could work with me."

"You will be fine Peter. Everyone brought you up for the role of Lord."

This was true and as Peter watched his brother leave, he thought about what he should do. Thomas and Reginald were both dear to him as was all his siblings, but the girls were happy and well married and beyond need of his help. But those two – how had it come to this?

The worry went from his mind for the next months as he took full control of the estates. The tenants and business men paid homage to the new Lord and Clarice could not have been happier. It was not until the following summer that she told him that she was now the head of the Mothecombe coven.

Peter had not been as involved as his father had in the coven. His mother Gilda was in her late sixties and in mourning. But, she was still agile and playing an active part in coven business. Gilda had been the head witch until Roger became ill a year prior and she had temporarily handed the reins over to

Anastasia Cwm, Isolda's mother, there being no one else suitable. This had not worked out well as Anastasia quickly made enemies and so a new leader had been sought.

Now Clarice had power and she asked that Peter come to a meeting and see just how she had progressed the coven. Peter was tempted to go but was a little frightened, though he would never have admitted the fact. He managed to put the meeting off for several months until Gilda took him to one side after the family had hosted a party one evening.

"I don't think I have long left on this earth Peter and I want to tell you a story before it is too late."

"Mother, you do not have to tell me anything that you don't want to," answered Peter, terrified that he was about to hear something he had managed to not know perfectly well to date.

"Sit here Peter," and Gilda patted the oak bench which gave them a great view of the moonlit rippled river which they both knew curled out of their sight through the willow branches before it reached the sea. It was a lovely warm night and the stocks smelled wonderful.

"Clarice tells me that she can't get you to see her at the meetings. She is very proud of her position and you should be too."

"I am proud of her, it's just that..."

"You are scared, I know baby. You were always scared of the dark and especially if I came home in my robes."

"I hardly remember that. I just know that some of the friends that you and father had and brought back to the house would frighten me sometimes."

"In what way?"

"Oh, I remember I would sneak out on to the landing and peep through the banister rails and look down, they would talk about the Devil and demons in the chapel in the woods and casting spells. I heard about mermaids and giant sea creatures and if I ever mentioned anything to Father he told me that I shouldn't have been listening."

"I see. It is all true you know. And that is what I want to talk to you about."

There was silence between them for a moment as they watched a merchant boat make its way back to sea. A sailor waved to them and they both waved back and Peter thought fondly of his childhood when they would all wait to wave to the boats and score points for each wave returned.

"I know that witchcraft works and that you can cast spells good or bad. What I don't understand is, why the need to get involved in the first place?"

"Silly boy. Power, influence, money and excitement."

She cuddled him and he let her.

"Now that Clarice has made it to the top of the tree, she will want to change the way the coven is run and you know why she wants to do that?"

"No."

"Because she doesn't understand any of it. She thinks spell craft is about chanting some words and beheading cockerels and mixing blood with frog's eyes."

"And it's not?"

"No. It's about having the knowledge and understanding it. Not many do and I want you to understand it before I leave here to join the rest of the family."

"Are you not feeling well? You aren't going anywhere yet, are you?"

"Not just yet, but I shall be one day and it is imperative that I pass on the understanding to you so that you can in turn."

"Is this something to do with Geoffrey?"

"He brought back the information from Richard who had secreted it in his tomb."

"How did Geoffrey find it then?"

"That has been written down too so that the stories cannot be forgotten."

"Where is all this stuff kept? I've never found it."

"It's all in the library. We can go and look now or tomorrow morning, but we need to do it soon. It will take you a while to learn and understand properly."

The sea had become very quiet, no boats, no early fishermen and they had not been disturbed by any person. It was very late and the moon was showing them that it was bedtime from self-respecting people.

"Why not now?" asked Peter. "We shall be pestered and bothered by everyone tomorrow and I would like to know these family secrets."

Gilda seemed pleased and held his arm tightly as they made their way back to the house across the dampening grass. They could see dim lights reflecting against the hall windows and knew that these had been left by the servants for their return. They also knew that there would be Thomas, an old retainer, sitting on the oak bench in the porch and waiting for them. It was also highly likely that he would be asleep.

They crept past the sleeping man and made their way to the kitchen for a hot drink to take to the library. Gilda brought out cake and then sent Peter ahead as she went back to nudge Thomas and tell him that it was now safe to lock up and go to bed.

Peter had riddled the fire - enough to get a blaze going and Gilda was glad of it.

"Thomas has gone up now. He was most disturbed that he hadn't noticed us coming in."

"Thomas is getting old. We need a younger man on the door."

"We will never find a more loyal man. Let him continue, the spells keep us safe."

"If the spells keep us so safe, how come Reginald lost his fiancée and we lose members of our family?" He riddled harder.

"Silly boy Peter. We never lose anyone, they only go into another place."

"Do we all go into the same place when we die? I mean whether we have chosen the 'correct' religion, or whether we just go about our business and never refer to God?"

"Yes, but it is a difficult question which requires a complicated answer…" she began.

"That is an easy way to say that you don't know the answer."

"No, that's not true. If your question was, will I be able to speak German one day, then I could answer in the same way. I would explain that although you know speaking German is possible and you know all the letters of the alphabet, you must still go through a process of practice and understanding before you succeed."

"I suppose," answered Peter, in a surprisingly sulky way.

"Sit down over there and I will bring you a book."

Peter did as he was told and watched his mother walk over to the wall and fiddle with one of the shelves. He loved this room and came here often when he wanted a break from his responsibilities. The walls were lined with books of all descriptions. There were record books of everything that had ever happened on the estate and details of every person who had ever lived there or dealt with the family. There were records from Orcherton and other Devon properties and the holdings and manors in Cornwall. Each tenant must give full details of their family and history in order to get a cottage or a job. Business dealings when recorded, also detailed the people involved and the family now had so much paperwork that one of the walls was completely occupied with them.

No one outside of their trusted staff knew about these. The documents were hidden behind calf leather and oak bindings and were too numerous to be noticed individually. This was the wall along which Gilda was running her hand. As she came to one section, there was a flash and a glow and Gilda removed the books from that particular section and laid them on the table. Peter left his chair and took hold of the books, bringing them all back carefully to the low table by the fire, which already held their refreshments.

When Gilda settled opposite him, she pointed to the top book and Peter obediently took hold of it and opened it carefully.

"Read it," instructed Gilda.

Peter began reading and Gilda leaned across and tapped his hand.

"Out loud Peter. You will understand it better then."

Peter grumbled but obeyed.

This is a true account of the teachings given to me by The Priestess at her cottage in the Pridias woods. I recommend that these teachings be read over and over again and thought about when going about your daily business. You may find that other people will not understand what these teachings refer to and so for that and many other reasons, I suggest that you do not discuss their content with anyone else.

"How much of this do I have to read?"

"More than you have so far. I will tell you when to stop." Gilda was leaning back in her chair, eyes closed and a smile on her face.

"Hmmm."

She has told me so many things that I find it difficult to put them in order. I don't think that it is necessary to practice the teachings in any particular order. I certainly didn't. I think that it is a matter of practicing and dedicating time to understanding and eventually it is just that. The understanding brings belief and belief brings conscious results rather than unconscious results.

He looked up and recognised that his mother was asleep and so he got up and covered her with a large fur blanket. She stirred slightly and snuggled down in the chair. Peter returned to his own chair, now interested in his book. He whispered the words, not wanting to upset his dear mother.

It seems that the only thing we must understand is that we are all God. He is not separate to us nor above us. He is not to be worshipped from afar, but to be acknowledged as the whole of which we are a part. If we want to possess something and encounter an experience, God already knows it and is willing to grant it. Praying is nothing more than an instruction to God to grant your desire and never, I repeat never, an incantation that must be said in the right order and at the right time before God decides whether or not He will answer your prayer. It is impossible to have a desire that cannot be granted. Impossible to have a thought that will not come true. But, be aware that God does not care whether you wish for evil or good, He will grant it regardless.

Firstly – Be careful and conscious of your thoughts

Secondly – Be aware that you can affect the actions and thoughts of another with your own thoughts.

Thirdly – Remain focussed at all times.

Fourthly – What you are doing to others, you are doing to yourself.

Fifthly – Nothing exists outside of yourself

Sixthly – If you want something, believe you already have it and never direct your thoughts in an opposite direction to your fulfilled wish.

Seventhly – All wishes come true.

Peter stopped reading. There were many more pages to go yet and an initial flick through showed him that these contained detailed instructions on how to achieve the focus. Was this how his mother achieved her notoriety and success in spell craft? Were all spells nothing more than concentrated thought? He leant back in his own chair, pulled a fur rug over his body and drifted into sleep.

He woke with a start and noticed that Gilda had already gone to bed. The fire was out, but Gilda had apparently lit some candles and by the light of these, Peter could see that the books were still on the table. He reached for them and turning the pages of the three he had not read, he noticed that the contents had been written by other hands than the original. The books contained spells and the results of spells and there were illustrations on many pages.

Peter looked back at the first book and saw that the pages had originally been part of long rolls which had been cut and bound in the oak and leather in which it sat. He felt the silver ornate corner pieces and read the name Lord Richard de Pridias on the front which had been embossed in gold leaf. It was beautiful and he hugged it to him as he suddenly remembered the story of its discovery as told to him by his late father.

It was the knocking at the library door which took him out of his musings. He slowly got up and moved to the door and was strangely nervous. The knocking was so insistent and unusual – that was the problem, he suddenly realised. He didn't recognise the knocking and if it was a stranger, how had he got as far as the library door?

The light from the hallway reflected feet moving, very large feet with odd, long toed shoes such as he had never seen. He put out his hand to open the door and realised that the handle was too high up. He could reach it, but now he had to reach up and not down as he had earlier that evening. He looked down and saw that he was dressed as a boy and a boy ready for bed. He scurried over to the ornate mirror hanging opposite the windows and saw that he was no taller than three and a half feet, perhaps less. He was carrying the Richard de Pridias book and it covered the whole of his torso and suddenly felt very heavy. He dropped it and the crashing noise it made as it hit the floor stopped the knocking and the feet ceased their shuffling.

Peter held his breath and when the door began to open, he ran behind it, ensuring that he would be hidden from whatever monster might be about to enter the room. The creature man shuffled in, bent over and his right arm crooked and holding on to his lower back. He swung each leg to the side before he moved it forward, making his progress slow and menacing. He grumbled and grunted and looked about him. The light from the hallway spread behind the creature, exaggerating and elongating his shadow across the room. He turned and Peter shrank back into the darkness as the creature's head pointed full on his direction. Peter saw dark, shiny eyes, huge and almond shaped, flicking from side to side. There appeared to be no whites in those dreadful eyes. The nose was thin and pointed and the mouth thin and large. It opened his mouth, drawing grey lips over ugly, short and sharp teeth.

It seemed that Peter was safe from his gaze, with the hallway light in the creature's eyes and Peter in the dark shadow. When the creature turned back to the room, Peter slipped out of the doorway and ran along the hallway. He must find his mother and have her help him.

He ran up the stairs and along the corridor to his parents' room. He didn't knock as he would usually have done, instead bursting in and running towards the bed. He drew back the curtain and shouted,

"Mama, Mama! A monster in the library!"

There was no answer. The bed was empty and still made up and Peter began to cry. This must be a dream – he could clearly remember being an adult not very long ago.

There were voices on the landing and Peter jumped on to the bed and drew the curtains, breathing erratically. This feeling of fear felt familiar and he half remembered being here before. He pushed himself under the blankets and shivered.

"How did it manage to find its way here?" A woman was talking as she entered the bedroom.

"My dear, my dear, I do not know. But I suspect it is something to do with Anastasia."

"Yes, she has always used the teachings for ill. I am glad that she doesn't know them in their entirety."

"Perhaps, but she is doing enough damage only knowing a part. I hadn't realised that she was conjuring a monster in her own woods. The stupid, stupid cow."

The woman threw a cloak on an oak chest and turned to the man accompanying her. Peter saw that is was his father and he let out a cry.

"Papa! Oh Papa!"

"Did you hear that noise?" asked Roger of his wife.

"I did. It sounded as though it was coming from the next room."

"I thought it came from in here. I thought that it sounded like little Peter."

"No, he should be abed with the other children. The maids would know if he was missing."

"They would."

"Mama! Papa! I am here!"

"I heard it again!"

"So did I, Roger."

Peter struggled with the curtains, desperately trying to open them, but they would not.

"Mama! Papa!" he cried.

"Why are the bed curtains moving so?" asked Roger.

Gilda took a sharp inward breath and rushed to her bed. She drew the curtains back and cried,

"Nothing here."

"We must be imagining it," said Roger.

"No, we are not. This is all part of the conjuring. Anastasia has bewitched us all."

"Even the children?"

"Peter anyway. He is the heir after all," added Gilda.

"And you think she wants to hurt him?"

"Confuse him, then she can control him later. We both know it has happened before."

Peter listened and drew back the curtains and ran towards his parents. It soon became obvious that he was invisible to them and he stood by the door, sobbing. How was he to save himself from this sorry state? Gilda had said that he was bewitched and he dreaded living through his childhood again.

"Listen," said Gilda sharply.

There were shuffling noises on the stairs and all three rushed to the landing. The creature was making its slow and swinging way up the stairs. Peter was terrified, he now knew that his parents were unable to help him. The dark, cloaked shape made its slow way through the gloom of the candlelight. Peter ran in front of his mother and stood at the head of the stairs.

The creature stopped too and stared at Peter.

"He can see something, Roger," said Gilda.

"Yes. Perhaps its Peter."

The creature had a quicker turn of speed and made it to the top before anyone expected. It stood in front of Peter and raised his arms. The cloak sleeves dropped back and the claw like hands lunged for him. Gilda sprung from her position by the banister rail and stood between Peter and the creature.

"Go back from whence you came," she snarled at the creature. "Leave my family alone and find comfort in the family of your creator!"

She closed her eyes and stood still.

"Stop the world," she said. "Change it. Now move on."

The creature dropped his arms and stood still.

"Leave us," added Gilda.

The creature turned and made his lumbering way down the stairs.

"Well done, my dear," praised Roger.

"Peter is here," said Gilda.

Peter turned to Gilda and threw his arms around her waist.

"I love you my boy," she said.

Roger and Gilda moved towards their room and Peter watched them go. He knew instinctively that he must return to the library if he was to return to his adult life. He sprinted down the stairs and towards the library door. From the corner of his eye, he saw the creature lumbering towards the front door and a younger Thomas shooing him out with a long broom.

Peter ran into the library and towards the chair. Then he got up, picked up Richard's book and shut the door before returning to his chair. He closed his eyes and waited.

He must have waited a long time, for he fell asleep and was woken by Thomas.

"You alright Sir? You must be cold sitting here all night."

"No, I'm not cold. I am fine." Peter patted himself down, relieved to see that he was now an adult again.

He stood up as Gilda came into the room.

"Mama!" he said without thinking.

"Ah! You have remembered Peter," said Gilda. "Fetch us refreshment Thomas, would you?"

"Yes, my Lady," answered Thomas and he left the room.

"I was a boy again."

"The spell is broken now Peter. Anastasia can no longer affect the family. So many deaths and misfortune just recently. She killed young Marjery, but never tell Reginald. He will see her again. And she bewitched Thomas to marry that hag of a daughter of hers. I had to cast an emergency spell on Thomas after your father left him property, she would have used it against us. But we are safe now that we have come full circle."

"I read some of the book, Mama."

"And you must read more and learn. These teachings can be used for good or ill, but you must be prepared for it to come back to you as creator. The ill was sent back to Anastasia and will have reached her today. The harvest is upon her now that you have been back in your mind and remembered."

Thomas came back into the room carrying a tray filled with a jug, goblets and plates of food.

"Thank you, Thomas," said Peter. "Thomas, I wanted to say how much we recognise the care you bestow on our family. It is very much appreciated."

Thomas blushed and said, "No more than I want to do, my Lord. The Pridias family have always been very good to me and mine."

Peter nodded and Gilda smiled.

"Oh, I almost forgot!" said Thomas.

"What's that?" asked Gilda.

"Anastasia Cwm died in the night. It came as quite a shock to the family it seems, as she had not been unwell. Came out of the blue, they say. Apparently, she woke in the night screaming that a creature was banging on her bedroom door. When the maid went in, Mrs Cwm dropped down dead."

"Oh, that is dreadful," said Peter.

"Hmmm," said Gilda. "She shouldn't have planted seeds in the world that she was not prepared to see bloom."

"Do we have no control over what blooms from another's seed, Mama?"

"No, but we can choose our reaction and that overcomes and changes that which we wish had not been planted. Come to a coven meeting with Clarice and I, you will learn more there. And read the teachings and tell no one of them except your first born. Not Clarice. She will not understand."

"Yes Mama."

"Listen to your Mama," added Thomas. "I have seen what she can do."

ICE DAY AT SEQUERS BRIDGE

Featuring Sir Roger de Pridias (1294-1347)

Winter has begun early and is achingly cold.

This was the first diary entry I read which seems relevant to the events that followed. Such strange events, the result of which I have neither seen nor heard the like before or since.

I am Sir John Pridias, son of Sir Roger de Pridias and Elizabeth Treverbyn of Cornwall. We are Cornish men and women, although we own more lands now in Devon than in Cornwall. My elder brother Sir Roger the heir inherited…. Well, I am running ahead of myself here. There is a lot to say before I get there. My wife Joan is the daughter and heir of Gilbert Adeston and I have upon my marriage three years ago become heir to two large properties south of Modbury which join with the lands of my family and if my brother. Now, I must continue with the diary entries of my father in order that the story will make sense to you. It doesn't make sense to me and so I am asking for your help.

Monday: I noticed the brook icing up when I rode across Sequers Bridge today. That is a very unusual occurrence and I mentioned it to a man carrying sacks of something or other as we passed on the bridge. He said that it was a sign that this winter would one of the worst we would see. I thanked him for his cheerful forecast and he clicked his pony on, not understanding my wit. I stood there for a few minutes and watched as the ice crackled in from the banks towards the centre of the stream. I thought that it would soon become difficult for the boats to come up and down and bring much needed products along the Erme and from the sea or Ermington.

Wednesday: I rode down to the bridge again today and the ice was moving in further. The trees are covered in a thick hoarfrost this morning and the birds are struggling to find food. There are still berries about the bushes, but seem too frozen for them to peck at. As I stand, my horse becomes impatient and cold I suspect. He paws at the ground and chips at the ice with his hooves. I did wonder whether I should ride on the road in case we should slip, but have stuck to the verge where I can. A rabbit runs out from the hedge and I watch it scurry away. Philip, one of my gamekeepers tells me that the poachers are becoming braver and less discreet as they became hungry. Some poachers are selling because they need money and others because their families are hungry. I must judge them when they are brought to court and I find it difficult to be cruel. Then a young fox ran across the bridge and caught the rabbit and I heard it squeal so dreadfully. I felt ill for the rest of the day.

Sunday: There has not even been the reprieve of snow. We are quite warm at the Hall and so are the servants, but there are some homeless and poor cottagers who are finding it very difficult to manage. I was told about a man who had been found frozen to death on the road and they couldn't move him because of the ice. So, they had to chip at him with an axe until he moved. Horrible.

Tuesday: It was a moonlit night last night and when I looked out of my window at the garden the view was that of a dream. Everywhere was white and black, softened by grey. A large owl, a Tawny, flew from an elm and landed on something, a mouse or a weasel perhaps and ate it whole. I looked back at Elizabeth sleeping solidly` in the bed. The wine she drinks before she retires every night helps her sleep. I know many do not sleep together when they have been married for so many years, but even after 25 years together I cannot sleep unless her body is beside me. I put on my coat and went downstairs and outside. No one saw me leave. The cold that hit me as I left the front porchway almost stopped my breath and I pulled my fur scarf over my face. I was going to fetch my horse, but decided that would be too much fuss and walked along the trackway instead. I could see Sequers Bridge across the fields and it looked white against the dark sky. I suspect it was the reflection of the moon. The owl screamed and flew past my ear in search of further titbits. It made me feel peculiar and I carried on with my walk with a heightened sensation of – anxiety – I think it was. I could see the ice on the brook as I neared it and as the wind picked up, the ice collected and blew towards me in such a strange way that I stopped in my tracks. Then there came a bright light in the sky, a huge light and I felt so sick and my head banged.

Saturday: I wrote Tuesday's entry just now as today's entry will make no sense without it. They tell me that I have been missing since Wednesday morning, when Elizabeth did not find me abed with her. All I can remember is the bright light and the owl and then waking up on the bridge. A man from the village found me and brought me home and they think I am suffering from some sort of mental decay because I don't know where I have been. I am now in bed with a hot pan and broth and ale on a tray until I recover. My son is here too. Roger that is. He is with his second wife Joan who is a Clifford and a cousin of his first wife. They have five children to add to his three from Elizabeth, but she died after birthing the last child, Edith. Peter and John are his boys from her and Peter is his heir. Then he has Alice, Johan, Elizabeth, Anne and Agnes with Joan. They are all under five years old and I don't know how his wife manages. Although I must admit that the maids look after them all and Elizabeth spends her day laying on a couch in her room whether with child or without. But, the women have brought to the family great areas of land adjacent to ours and we must be thankful for that. John is not currently here, he has business with his wife's family, the Adestons. That girl has brought to the family lands which are adjacent to ours too. The wives are not Cornish and I am not terribly happy about that, but they have brought wealth and property and in this modern world we cannot have everything it seems. I will stop now so that I may sleep. I am so very tired and the weather is still so very cold.

Wednesday: I have slept so much and had such terrible dreams. I am still abed and not allowed up until the weekend. My servant John, washes me with a cloth and changes my bedding while rolling me from side to side. I am not sure why, although I do feel so weak and my heart rattles and speeds at such speeds. I see frost on the windows and sometimes on the inside too. John scrapes the ice off telling me that there never has been such a winter and its only November! It makes me anxious to see the ice and I go back to my nightmares. I dream of flying chariots which come from - I don't know where – and take me back to their lair where they would – and there I cannot remember what happens next. I started to tell Elizabeth and she had such a shocked look on her face and talked about the Devil and his demons and how I was describing things which God would not approve. It has not been pursued with me as to where I was for those days though. No one has asked me nor mentioned it and that is odd in itself.

Sunday: Roger has accompanied me on a visit to Sequers Bridge. Both of our wives had begged that we should not go, but I insisted. As my mind cleared, I was adamant that I had done nothing other than go for a night-time walk in the ice and yes – I remembered the ice as it blew froth-like towards me and then the owl and the bright light. Roger says that I must have mistaken the moon for the light and even when I explained how the light had made it impossible to see anything other than the light, they did not believe me. The horses took us down the drive to the road and then turned southwards towards the bridge. We passed the gatekeeper at the front door of his cottage and he shouted that we should take great care on the roads because of the thick ice. Roger dutifully slowed the horses down and we ambled to the bridge. I pulled my rug tighter and higher as the ice was so terrible we could hardly breathe. When we stopped at the bridge crown, I pointed out where I had seen the light, halfway between the bridge and the hall. Now, the brook is frozen across and white. The trees overhanging is solid with ice and the overhanging branches are frozen into the water. Ducks stagger along the surface and stare hopelessly at the shadows of frozen fish beneath the surface. My son tells me that the boats are no longer able to come upstream from above Mothecombe with even the river current being stopped by the thick ice. The ice from the River Erme was blowing out to the sea on the outgoing tide and even the mermaids were stuck in their undersea homes. We should come at night, I told him. Perhaps we would see the white light then. Roger seems disappointed that I have not remembered what happened to me during those days and I expect he thinks I was laid up in some cottage with a comely woman. I was not.

Tuesday: I have persuaded Roger to come out with me after supper to see if there would be any sign. He was reluctant in front of his wife, but excited and interested I believe. Peter, my grandson wanted to come too and with promises to look after him, Peter was wrapped up and added to the mission. The night was darker than before and the thick clouds held a promise of snow. Peter was excited at the prospect while Roger said that his hunting would be upset if it did snow. We arrived at the bank of the brook and waited. The ice was thicker than before and it is very strange. Peter suddenly screamed that he could see a huge white object in the sky – much bigger than an owl or a bird. We looked and gracious me! A round building hovering in the sky and we could not work out whether it was over the land or the sea. We stared at it and noticed a light streaming downwards from it which proved that it was further away from us than we thought. The horses were impatient and we decided to return to the Hall. There was the most peculiar feeling in the air, like just before a big thunderstorm and yet the weather is completely wrong for that to be the case. When we arrived home, both Peter and Roger were nervous, I could tell.

I have refrained from transcribing several of Roger's entries as I can summarise without breaking momentum. The weather became worse and the snow fell, lying feet thick in some places. Roger and his son and grandson became ill and were sent to their beds to recover. It was assumed that they had some kind of paralysis from their ventures on a cold night. They were delirious and talked of gods and chariots in the sky. They were not believed. There was also much discussion about the number of animals that were going missing, considered the result of poachers in this difficult winter. Horses and cattle were gone and also a family who rented a cottage on the edge of the Orcherton estate and a couple near Bigbury. They had left their four children who were taken to the church and placed with their aunt and uncle until their parents returned. So far, no one had returned and there had been no word and so the poaching was laid at their door. I have transcribed again from 9th February 1347 when the weather was still atrocious.

Thursday: There is no longer anytime for laying in our beds. This is the weather of doom with the constant ice and thick snow. People and animals are starving and there are more and more sightings of the strange chariot in the sky. Sometimes it appears in the daylight in addition to the night and more people are seeing it. Ships at sea have watched it swoop along the waves and then below the sea and vanishing. It has also to be said that in addition to families vanishing and a great deal of people dying, I do not and cannot believe, that it is solely to do with the bad weather. Unless of course, the chariot has something to do with this bad weather. Our family has been ill and I have insisted that my other son, John and his family do not visit us because Roger and his younger daughters especially, have not been well of late.

Monday: I have just been visited today by some of my neighbours. The rich and landed ones naturally. It is not considered appropriate for me, a Knight of the County to be announcing the second coming of Christ or angels. Members of the clergy have said that is what I am about, although I know for a fact that two of my neighbours and one of the Rectors who was mentioned to me have seen the chariot for themselves. I suspect that I am being used as a scapegoat in case everything turns out to be an illusion. I explained again what I saw and said that I will only ever speak the truth and answer to my Maker accordingly. There was a much harrumphing, but they left in a good mood. I haven't told them that my memory has been coming back and I have an inkling that I have been on board the chariot. I am remembering some very strange sights of men and women dressed in a way I do not recognise and them speaking in our language, but with some differences. They were kind to me and told me about life travelling around space and time, I believe they said, although that made no sense to me. I remember talking about my family and they said I could go home. That is all I remember.

Friday: I remembered more today. They told me that I was going back with them to Lyonesse. Is Lyonesse the land of my ancestors? I think so. I must ask my son Roger. Still very cold and even we are getting hungry now.

Sunday: At church, I talked to more neighbours and the gossip is all about the harsh weather. It was so cold in the church that the font has frozen solid and there is ice inside the windows and on the inside of the doors. We all shivered and shook as the Rector babbled on about – I know not what – I was too busy thinking about that chariot. Perhaps that has come from God? Its mentioned in the Bible certainly. Old Bigbury told me that he has seen something in the sky, sending down to the sea a huge light which illuminated under the water and he said he thought that he saw a wrecked ship there. I don't know if that is true and yet I have never heard him lie. There were more people attending the service than usual today and I see a rise in anxiety in the congregation.

Thursday: My son Roger called to fetch me and took me to Sir William Bigbury's Hall as apparently, he wanted to show me something. We had an excellent dinner and when the women had left us, Sir William ordered his carriage and the three of us set off for the coastline, which is very close to his Hall. We took the lane which leads to the beach from where one can reach the island at low tide. That was to be at 2 am and so as we began our walk across the beach at midnight, we would have four safe hours in which to cross to the island and return. The three of us set off across the beach and soon reached the inn and cottages at the base of the island. Lights flickered inside, but saw no one apart from a man quickly opening the door and peering round. Upon seeing his master walking with his friends, he nodded and went back inside and dropped the bar on his door. Sir William hurried us along, informing us that after midnight was the best time to see. To see what, we asked? Hurry along, he insisted and hurry we did. We were all quite breathless as we crowned the hill and looked out to sea. We saw nothing unusual other than ships sailing silently westwards and the dim lights of coastal cottages perched aloft the cliffs. We sat down on a bench there, huddled against the icy wind and drinking the wine brought by my son Roger. Just as we were about to begin our return, there was the most dreadful screeching sound and something huge passed above our heads and out to sea. When I say huge, I mean we could not see the sky at all as it passed over. The speed it went out to the horizon and then back to centre stage, I cannot describe adequately. We did not speak as we watched and I don't know how I shall ever explain what we saw to anyone else. It seems like a lie. I saw a huge white and grey carriage or chariot, the like of which I have never seen. Perhaps a sky-going ship without the sails – I think I will try and draw it. We could not take our eyes away from it and when a light came down from it into the sea, it was as though Heaven had opened and was beckoning souls to return. We wondered if that is what it is – the way we return to our Lord at the end of our life. I felt a strange energy in my stomach. Like when a carriage goes over a bridge too fast and there is a tickling sensation. I told Roger and Sir William of my memory of being told I was to return and go to my ancestors and Roger said that would be exciting and Sir William said it was a Devil's trick. Anyway, the light revealed shipwrecks and sea creatures before it suddenly switched off and then the chariot vanished. I thought it vanished, but Sir William said he was sure it just moved very quickly away. We had much to discuss on the journey home and were very surprised when the servants at Bigbury insisted that we had been gone for a night and a day. Roger said he felt very sick as did I and Sir William said he was going to go directly to his son's Hall in the north of the County as he had never felt so disorientated in his life.

And that was all. My father never made another entry in his journal as he sickened after that night and eventually died three months later. My brother Roger lasted a further month, but succumbed to the same wasting disease. The surgeons cannot decide whether it is because of the severe weather or an unknown sickness. We have heard that plague is moving up through Europe and perhaps some ship or merchant has brought it to our shores. Currently, the five younger children of Roger are very sick and Peter, his heir, is being made a ward of Walter de

Wodeland, a man of dubious honour. I have not shown the journal to anyone, feeling that it will only confuse the matter and will keep it instead in the oak chest in which many personal Pridias documents are kept.

Perhaps it was the chariot of our Lord.

I hope it was not the chariot of the Devil.

BIG, BLACK RATS

Featuring Sir John Pridias (1320-1357)

"No one likes rats."

"I think it is fair to take that as a given John," said Joan.

"I heard of one man in the village who keeps them as pets and trains them to fetch him food," answered her husband.

"Why would anyone want to eat food that a rat had fetched?"

"I have no idea," John said.

John and Joan had been married for thirteen years and had a twelve-year-old son, Giles. Joan's father Gilbert Adeston, owned huge tracts of land south of Modbury and as husband of his co heir, John was immensely rich. This situation was fortunate but had been planned. He was the second son of Roger de Pridias, who had died a few weeks following the death of his heir and John's elder brother Roger. In the weeks following, the deceased heir lost his youngest five children. Now, Roger's son and John's eldest nephew Peter, was under the wardship of Walter de Wodeland and the ancestral Pridias lands would be lost to John forever. Walter now wanted to wed his own daughter to Peter and as Walter had already married a female ward of his and gained her properties, he knew the game.

One of the servants, Alan, had recently entered the room and informed them that there were now so many rats around the stables and outbuildings, that they could not kill them quickly enough. The known rat catcher in the village was busy in the villages killing the unusually high number living in the church, cottages, woods and everywhere else.

"So, my Lord and my Lady, he won't be coming here to help us."

"That is such a nuisance," said Joan. "I said that they should not have killed so many cats and then we would not have the rats."

"Nor the plague and the Sweating Sickness. These rats carry it all."

"I am sure that something, a merchant ship or a foreign traveller, brought the infected rats with them and caused the deaths of so many of your family, John."

"Perhaps, perhaps. It is certain that we must kill more rats and kill them quicker if we want to rid our country of these dreadful diseases." He was thinking about the stories his father and brother had told him about the flying chariot.

Joan rose from her chair to stem the anxiety she felt. Rats, big ones in grey, black and brown roamed freely around. It was terrifying to take a walk when the ground could be carpeted at any time by the horrid creatures who had no hint of fear. They had no enemies other than terrier dogs or men with great clubs and these enemies appeared to constantly busy elsewhere. When she was a girl, Joan knew that rats mooched and nested about the barns and stables, but the cats and the men had kept them at bay. Now one never saw a cat and men who were willing to kill the rats.

"At least we don't have so many witches," commented John.

"Not in plain sight," answered his wife. She knew of the coven history of John's family, but said nothing.

"What shall I do now, my Lord?"

"Oh Alan, I do not know. We may have to lure them into a barn and sacrifice that to fire."

"Yes, my Lord," and he bowed.

"Off you go, I shall let you know."

The next afternoon, Joan was walking across the long meadow which led to Sequers Bridge. She was alone today and was wondering why she had not managed to conceive another child since Peter. She knew that neither she nor John had a problem – Peter was testament to that. She was wondering whether to visit the Mothecombe coven and ask there. She was sure that John's family had been involved in it but as it was a secret group, had no real confirmation of such. There must be an introduction in order to a have a question answered or a spell cast by them and she daren't ask John. No, he would not approve.

Her musings were disturbed by a scurrying noise in the reeds to her left.

"My Lady! Move yourself! Quick now!"

Move herself she did and with her heart beating fast, Joan Pridias leapt on to the cart from where her rescuer screamed. The ground upon which she had previously stood was coated with rats. Unbeknownst to her, rats had been following her steps as she meandered down the bank path and were being joined forward and back by their friends and family. The carter had noticed this as he moved at a distance behind her and had cantered his pony in order to reach her before the rats did. As Joan hurled herself into the seat alongside the driver, he grabbed her skirts and legs and threw her safely into the well of the cart. Then he whipped the air above his frightened pony and cantered across the meadow until they reached the driveway to the Hall.

Joan had held tightly on to the rails around the cart and managed to turn herself in spite of the bouncing. The driver pulled up on the drive and leant down to comfort his sweating, terrified pony.

"I apologise my Lady. I did not mean to frighten you and manhandle you in such a disrespectful way. But…"

"It was necessary and I am grateful that you rescued me. I shall see that you are rewarded well by my husband."

"I did not do it for that, my Lady. I did not want you hurt like the people in the village and cottages. Have you heard that rats are now killing babies which have been left unattended and that they are biting and attacking anyone?"

"No! No, I have not and I am alarmed to hear about such a dreadful thing! Why do we have so many just now?" Joan was brushing her skirts with her gloved hands and realised that she had an urge for a pee, but naturally was unable to tell this stranger.

"I think that it is a mixture of things, my Lady. People have died from the plague, no cats about and more men going to work in the mines. There's more money there than working for rich families as servants."

Joan smiled, expecting the carter to realise his faux pas and apologise, but he did not.

"I will take you back home, my Lady and don't come out without a manservant and in a carriage until this problem has been sorted."

"Do you know how the problem must be solved?" she asked.

"Kill the damned lot of them! There is no use for a rat as far as I can see, other than food."

"Do people eat rats?" she asked, horrified.

The carter looked at her bemused, "Starving people do, my Lady. Starving people do."

Joan remained quiet until she was at the door of the Hall. Her rescuer insisted that she stay aboard until he had fetched help. He knocked sharply at the front door and ignored the scowling look from Alan, when he saw him.

"I have your Lady here. She has had a shock and I brought her home. I wish to see his Lordship while I am here," he insisted.

"I do not know if my Lord is at home," sniffed Alan.

"Yes, you do and he is. I need to see him."

"It is alright Alan," said Joan. "Help me down and then fetch my husband."

John listened to the morning's events and sighed heavily.

"Something must be done," he said. "And quickly."

Joan listened quietly and when the carter, Thomas Black, had left, said to her husband,

"Can the coven help?"

He looked at her and answered,

"I am going to ask."

It was not until the following day, that John told her as they ate breakfast,

"I have spoken to the coven. I shall not upset you with the details, my dear, but they are to do something and I have promised to help."

"Will it be dangerous?" Joan asked.

"There is always an element of danger Joan. But we must accept that to allow these rats to roam free, is hugely dangerous. I cannot bear to imagine what could have happened to you if that carter had not rescued you."

"I cannot bear to think of it myself John. I am not sure that I dare go out alone now."

"You must not go out alone and do not allow Giles to either."

"Not even with his dog?"

"Not at all. We shall send servants for anything needed and no one will go out alone."

Joan shivered as she looked out of the huge windows and saw packs of rats moving together, unaffected by the servant who was throwing stones at them. She did not want her breakfast now.

The household was raised in the middle of the night by the banging of the door and the ringing of the bell. As John and Joan lifted their heads from their pillows, they tensed against the terrible screams they heard. John jumped from his bed and covered himself with his cloak. He picked up the lamp and hissed to his wife,

"Make sure Giles is safe and then lock yourselves in his room," before he left the bedchamber.

Joan cloaked her body and ran across the landing, then up the stairs to Giles room. He was awake and white-faced.

"Mama! What's happening?"

"I don't know, Giles. Your father and the servants are dealing with it. We are to remain locked in here."

Giles stood straight and said,

"I will protect you Mama."

He double bolted both doors and opened the curtains so that he could check the window locks.

"Look Mama," he said.

Joan climbed onto the window seat and looked out. There were several people running about the drive way and in the trap, was a woman holding two children close to her. The lamps hanging from the trap illuminated two rearing horses and a servant trying to calm them.

"There are things running under the horses' feet," squealed Joan.

"They are rats!"

"Oh, my Lord! They are running up the horses' legs and the trap!"

Suddenly the servant could no longer hold the horses and they kicked and galloped back up the driveway, lamps swinging and rats being flung right and left. The screams of the woman and children could be heard even through the locked windows until the noise dimmed as they went from view.

"There is Papa! Oh, do be careful Papa!"

John was on the drive way with the visitors and they saw Alan and other servants. They were dancing and smashing the ground with their sticks and the rats were running towards them and filling in the ground where they had been dancing. Rats always ran away! But these rats were not!

"John! Get inside!" screamed Joan as she began to rattle the window and open it.

"No Mama! Don't!"

Giles pulled at his mother and slammed the window shut just as a large black rat plopped onto the outside sill from the little gable roof above the window. He was joined by another and another and as Joan screamed, they stood on their hind legs and tried to smash the glass with their pointed scratchy paws. Giles imagined how those pointy nails would feel upon his body and almost fainted.

"Mama, stop making such a noise. They are attracted to it."

Joan shut her mouth and put her hand over it to prevent a recurrence.

"I am sorry Giles. I am a little in shock I think."

He kissed her and then set about reinforcing the window with the heavy wooden shutters generally only closed on the coldest of evenings. He lit more lamps and candles and instructed,

"Make sure there are no weaknesses in the room Mama."

This task busied their bodies and their minds and it seemed that no weakness could be found.

"I have been hearing rats scratching at the panels the past few nights, Mama!" confessed Giles.

"Did you tell the servants? Your father?"

"I told Papa and he said that he was dealing with it and that I was not to worry."

Their whisperings were stopped when they heard John outside the door.

"My dears!"

"Oh John, what is happening?"

"It's the rats. They are attacking the houses. Not just ours, everyone's house."

"Who was that? In the trap with the children?"

"They are the Bigbury's. William Bigbury is still here, but the trap horses ran away with his wife and children. We are getting a party together to rescue them."

"Papa, rats have been trying to get in through the windows."

"Giles, I need your help. Make sure your mother is safe and then ensure the whole Hall is safe from rat intrusions. The coven is sorting something out as we speak and hopefully the problem will be finished by morning."

"Yes Papa. Please take care of yourself." He began unlocking the door and John shouted,

"Keep your mother safe!"

The door opened and Joan ran out and hugged her husband.

"I have a bad feeling John. I wish you would stay here with us."

He held her arms and answered,

"I must do my duty Joan. You know that."

"We should be your duty father, not the Bigburys."

A look passed between them and John clicked his heels together and bowed to the pair of them before he turned and ran down the stairs. As the front door slammed Giles stood at the stop of the stairs and said,

"Mama, you lock yourself back in and I shall secure the Hall."

"I will not Giles. You go downstairs and begin there. Make sure all doors and windows are secure and I shall do up here after I make sure the servants are busy too. Do not worry, the Hall is built solidly and rats have only entered before through an opening and not the wall or foundations."

They busied themselves, locking doors and windows, bolting shutters and boosting the fires in all the chimneys. The remaining servants, mainly women, helped and they were soon done. Joan and her son went back upstairs and placed themselves behind shutters in the largest window.

The could see a lamplit group making their way down the driveway and another larger group, also lamplit, coming towards them from the direction of the driveway gatehouse.

"It's the Mothecombe coven," said Joan.

When John shut the front door behind him, he also had a bad feeling. He wondered if he would be coming home again and so he swiftly shook the thought from his mind. The tousled group in front of him consisted of Sir William Bigbury, his servants and

John's own servants. Bigbury was hysterical and pleading for help with his family.

"Why did you bring them here on such a night?" asked John.

"Because man, we were travelling home from Modbury and when the bridge was blocked with rats and such, I decided to bring them to your Hall for safety!"

"Yes, yes, I see. We will go and find them and bring them back here. I have reinforcements coming over at midnight."

"Who?" asked Bigbury.

"The coven."

The rats had been temporarily spooked by the runaway trap, but were now gaining confidence and returning to the group. John had the servants hand out flaming torches and they began to try and set fire to the rats. Apparently, rats are not terribly flammable and the torches only served to move them further away.

They decided against horses and instead walked down the drive in the direction of the horse and trap. John could soon see that the lit coven was moving towards them from the drive entrance. There was a faint chanting and melodic singing and in response to this, the group walked faster.

The rats were closing in on them again and surrounded their feet and scampered over the top of their boots and began running up their legs. Grown men screamed and squealed as they smashed torches and sticks against their own bodies. The rats reached shoulders and heads and the men grappled with them, throwing one or two to the floor which were replaced by another two or three. They were being overrun and overpowered.

The singing became louder as the coven almost reached them and the rats stopped moving. They suddenly fell from the men like wasps who had been sprayed with vinegar and lay curled on their backs and squealed and screamed. It was horrible.

The chanting and singing continued and the rats on the driveway and the meadow ran towards them and as they neared, they fell on their backs and died a terrible death. Rats came from the house and the stables and the river and fell and died. It took half an hour before the rats stopped coming and there was a carpet, several rats high as far as they could see. To move was to walk across still squirming, furry bodies which squeaked and cried as they were trodden on.

"My family?" asked Bigbury.

The hooded coven leader, slowly shook her head and Bigbury fell to the ground sobbing. But he soon rose again when he touched the squirming rats.

"Are you going to kill them all?" enquired John.

She nodded and turned and the coven moved away, chanting and singing.

"Alan, let us check on Sir William's family."

Alan nodded and they made their way to the upturned trap, still lit by lamps but missing the horses who had run well out of danger. It took a while, as they first must lift one foot above the corpses and then the other. The family were bloodied and rat covered and Alan knocked them away with his torch. John went forward and lifted the family up, one by one.

"The children are still breathing," he shouted and Sir William arrived to assist. He tried to raise the trap from the ground but was stopped by John.

"William, even if we manage to move the trap, we will never get it past the rat bodies."

"We must carry the children back to the Hall. Gently now."

And they did. They carried the children between them, sometimes carrying one and then passing it over to another man so they could have a breather. They were struggling to clamber over the rats, some of which still did not appear to be totally dead. They squeaked and almost drowned out the screams of their dying cousins who were currently being killed on the boundaries of their land. The lamp lit coven were visible and then invisible as they made their way over Sequers Bridge and down the road to Bigbury.

John thought about his meeting with her last night and the discussion of the rats. They agreed that the fear of witches had resulted in a cull of cats and a rise in the number of rats. There was a thought running through his mind now that the number of rats seemed inconsistent with the lack of cats. What was now to result from this catastrophe was the allowing of as many cats as anyone wanted, small and large. There was to be no limit and John knew full well that the coven wanted their cats back. Had this been a plan? By the coven? Had they spread the plague? And the chariot?

She laughed when he asked her that.

John felt ill and faint. Perhaps it was the result of tonight's shocks and the effort of carrying two dying children over heaps of dead rats.

"There is blood pouring from your neck my Lord," said Alan.

John put his hand to his throat and realised that he was losing a lot of blood. In fact, it was running river-like down his tunic. He just made it to the front door as Joan and Giles ran out.

"Help the children!" shrieked Sir William.

John fell on the big, black rats piled on the drive.

And died.

GHOST SHIP

Featuring Giles Prideaux (1345-1410)

Twenty-eight-year-old Sir Giles handed the documents to one of King Edward III Customs Officers as they sat opposite each other in the cleanest of the harbour inns.

"I see you have signed it Giles Prideaux. Why have you decided to change from de Pridias?"

"I decided a few years ago, when I became Burgess and MP for Totnes. My stepfather and father-in-law had been trying to persuade me that my proper name was reminiscent of old times and if I wanted to get on, I needed a modern interpretation."

"According to Hawley, others in your clan have changed to Prideaux too."

"Yes. My father and his ancestors would not approve, but we must survive and maintain our lands, whatever it takes."

"And is that why you have joined forces with John Hawley to relieve merchants of their cargos?"

"No. We are not pirates, we are merchants and businessmen. It is all in the documentation you hold in your hand."

"Hmmm. My master King Edward, has had complaints from his continental friends that cargos are being pirated and that businessmen from Dartmouth are to blame."

"It is not true. We are respectable men here, not pirates."

The Customs Officer read quickly and said,

"You are still maintaining that this was a ghost ship?"

"It was a ghost ship. I don't know what else it could be called."

The men said nothing further until another man joined their table.

"Aaah John, your man here is still determined that we are pirates."

"I find it difficult to think of a way to tell my superiors and betters that a ghost ship has been sailing our waters," said Customs.

"Not just one, they are often seen hereabouts," added Hawley.

"You should write fiction my friends. There are enough ideas here for plays and plays."

"Perhaps you can use us as characters in your own work."

"My scribbles, you mean? I doubt that anyone will ever read them!"

"I have read them and they are not too bad Geoffrey!" answered John.

Geoffrey Chaucer laughed and sat back in his chair,

"Well, Sir Giles Prideaux, let me hear the tale from your own mouth."

"To make you understand the tale in its entirety, I have to take you back to my childhood...," began Giles.

"Oh Lord, not that Giles! Geoffrey doesn't have to hear all the trimmings, just the facts!"

"You are wrong John. I want to hear everything. I like background and foreground. It is the only way to understand. Then I can trim the story to suit." Geoffrey poured more wine and beckoned to Giles.

"My father died when I was twelve and as I was the heir to his properties and those of Mama's, I was made ward of Simon Longbrooke, a neighbour of ours. He was a good man and his family had suffered with the plague and the rats as had mine. My mother remained Lord of Adeston until she handed over the whole property to me last year."

"My parents died of the plague and an uncle brought me up. That was why I was so determined to become rich and never rely on another," said John.

"Did your father die of plague Giles?" asked Geoffrey.

"No. He was killed and partially eaten by the giant rats that roamed our neighbourhood for a time."

"Oh! I had not expected that. How dreadful. And your mother?"

"She married John de Moel, a family friend from Cadbury. He was a very good man and looked after her and our properties very well, along with my father in law."

"And his name?"

"He was Simon Longbrooke. I married his beautiful daughter Isabelle," confessed Giles.

"A clever boy with a clever father in law. He managed to get your lands into his family coffers," said John.

"The properties are all in my name and everything will go to our children. Unlike my cousins, descended from the heir to Orcherton."

"What happened to them?" asked Chaucer.

"Cousin John killed Sir William Bigbury at Sequers Bridge near our home. There was an argument about how my father died and about the treatment of Bigbury's daughter. It began as an argument over who killed a deer and ended up in death. The King confiscated most of the properties that had been in our family for generations, but cousin John did not die."

"I bet the family were pleased about losing all that."

"Not really. It's a good job I have a lot of property, I suppose. But it takes much money to keep it all going, servants aren't what they were," said Giles.

"So, he came into business with me and we got him elected as Burgess and MP and we do some profitable business together. We import fancy goods and export tin and wool, but we do not steal," said John Hawley.

"And as we deal a lot with France, they pronounce my name as we say it now. Anyway, Mama became ill last year and handed all properties over to me. She sadly died a few months ago and is buried at home with the other members of my family."

"I am sorry to hear that. It is a terrible thing to lose your mother," said Chaucer.

"We none of us have living mothers I fear," added John. "Let us drink to them!"

And they did.

Giles continued.

"Now I am left with keeping the Houses of Adeston and Longbrooke running and paying all the bills. Hence my aforementioned diversion into business. Hawley and I have a usefully profitable business between us and ships are coming in and out all the time. It has been said that Hawley can take advantage of the wind, for he will always have a ship somewhere where the wind is favourable."

"I do, I do," agreed John.

"Then this one night a ship docked and told us of a ship they had seen drifting just outside the harbour. There appeared to be no one aboard and it was surrounded by a very unusual mist."

"Unusual? How?"

"They said that when they tried to tack over to the shop, they felt the same sensation as when a storm was about to occur. But there was no storm, it was a peaceful night, warm and calm. The crew did not attempt to board her, just came and told us. We organised a boat and took some men and sailed to where it had been seen. And we saw nothing."

Chaucer said, "No ship?"

"And no evidence. We thought the sailors must have been hysterical or drunk," added Hawley.

"Until the next time. It only took three days before two separate captains told us about a drifting ship with no crew. Both mentioned the peculiar mist and the feeling it gave them when they approached. Another week and five more sightings, yet no one had boarded and when the ship was specifically sought out, it was not to be seen."

"I am enjoying your story Giles Prideaux," said Chaucer. "I am taking mental notes."

"It is a tale of the truth Mr Chaucer and I hope that you are convinced by the time I have finished it," said Giles.

"If it is the truth, then I have no reason to stop listening."

"I hope not. Now, these sightings continued for more than two months and we left Spring and went into Summer. The light nights meant that locals could, during their leisure, take coast walks and as a result, the sightings increased. The ship was seen by many and the descriptions were all the same. A tall ship with flapping sails which was surrounded by a greenish mist that swirled and thickened as the ship moved. It sailed aimlessly across the sea and John and I were determined to board her and see what was there."

"So, we let it be known that we must be told as soon as the ship was spotted. I had a small schooner ready for immediate sail and stocked with necessities. We had no shortage of volunteers to jump when word was given," added John.

"And then one evening we were off! A family were having an evening picnic on the beach and they spotted the ship. They sent their lad back to the harbour and he ran into this very inn and told us the ghost ship was in view. We sprang into action and within minutes were on our way. The tide was with us and off we set. It was still light, although the orange sun was beginning to sink. The ghost ship was there, shrouded in a mist and we looked back to home to see that the coast line was becoming covered by sailors and locals and merchants as the news spread. It was very exciting and the wind brought us near to our goal and we chattered and got ready to snare the ship with our ropes and anchors. The mist, which had been thin, was now thickening again and spread its cold fingers on our direction. I felt almost over excited, drunk with anticipation until the fear came over me and I realised that fear was what I had been feeling all along."

"We all felt fear, it was the most bizarre thing. We sailed around the ship in a large circle in order to get nearer and as we lost contact with the mist, the fear went," interrupted John Hawley.

"But we continued. We had a short conversation amongst our crew about the danger, but we could see no one on board and curiosity had the better of us."

"I wish it was tonight, for I would sail with you," said Geoffrey Chaucer.

"I shall give you as much detail as possible and see if that is enough for you," said Giles. "Now I shall continue with my tale swiftly, for I have told my wife I shall be home at Adeston tonight. As we neared the ship, a rope with a large hook attached to the end was thrown over the side. It caught and we were able to throw on three more and secure it to our own ship. The mist still surrounded us and we all were fearful. I noticed that the ship was called *Borja* and I shouted its name as we climbed over the rails, but there was no answer. We left two men on our own ship and eight of us went aboard *Borja*. We held daggers and swords and split in twos so that we could explore quickly."

Hawley, listening intently, lifted the dagger which he had around his neck on a cord and Chaucer smiled and nodded. Giles continued,

"The mist was still surrounding us, but it was doing just that. Surrounding the ship and there was no sign of it aboard. I could no longer see the people along the coastline and the setting sun looked green. Whether that was the mist I do not know, for the sun has a tendency to turn into a green ball just before it falls off the horizon. We shouted and looked about, but saw nothing on the deck and so Hawley and I beckoned the others to go into the cabin and the hold. The tables were laid with food and there were plates and beakers about as though a meal had just been eaten. I am quite aware that ships such as this have been seen before, with talk that the crew perhaps fell ill or overboard. But it did not feel like that. It was as though the crew were still there and we could not see them. There were noises and mutterings but we could see no one. There was a shout from below and we went to see what had been found there. There were no people and no cargo. I didn't know then what was supposed to be aboard, but I am telling you that there was no cargo when we first went aboard. We went through the whole ship three times and found nothing that would intimate a person was or had recently been, on board. So, we went back on deck chattering amongst ourselves and agreeing to tow the ship to port. We could keep it until its owners were found."

"And perhaps claim it if they weren't," noted Chaucer.

"Perhaps, but it wasn't to be that simple. When we looked over the side, our own ship had gone, sailed back to port to catch the tide, we assumed. However, one of our men pointed out that it was now daylight and that the coastline looked 'a bit funny'. It certainly did. There were more people on the beaches and many seemed to have colourful tents or flags of some kind. There were people in the water and then we noticed the boats! Small ones with a colourful sail which carried a standing person dressed in black, swaying to and fro. Some large boats had sails too and some had no sails at all, but were steered by handles and cut through the waves very quickly. We shouted out and a couple came over to us and laughed and joked when we asked their names. They seemed to think that we were actors or jokers and they said that we were very good. We could get nothing more from them and I am afraid I did not ask too much as I was quite shocked at how little these people were wearing. The men wore nothing more than big pants and the women were practically naked. Two little bits of fancy string about their loins and breasts and no one seemed bothered! Some of those women were beautiful..."

"And some not so much..." added Hawley.

"We tried to leave the ship by throwing a boat over, intending to climb into it, but as soon as it hit the water it vanished. We were in magical realm we thought and decided that the only way out, was to collect the sails together and steer *Borja* back to port. We tried, oh we tried and it wouldn't work. We would set our course with all hands on deck and although we appeared to cross waves and tack towards the harbour, the coast remained the same distance away. Suddenly the mist dropped again and our new sights and sounds became blurred through it. My anxiety was rising and the crew began shouting at each other. Then a man who none of us knew suddenly appeared on the deck before us. He spoke Italian, I think it was and he seemed most agitated. We tried to get him to let us know what had happened to the rest of his crew and he pointed his palms to the air as if he couldn't understand and then began praying and crying. Then he vanished into the mist which swirled around him and the deck. I have to tell you that we were all very frightened by now because none of it made sense. The new peculiar scene had now vanished and we could see only the almost set sun through the mist. Then a shout of

'Ahoy!' made us look to the rails and there was our own ship with its skeleton crew asking us where in the hell we had been? We couldn't answer satisfactorily and they told us that we had vanished too. The ship had still been there but there had been no sign of us and they were about to leave and fetch help. We towed the *Borja* back to port and had it thoroughly looked over. There was definitely no cargo, no crew and no obvious explanation. If the Genoa friends of the King are saying that we stole the cargo and killed the crew, then they are mistaken."

"Do you seriously think that if I tell them this story, they will believe it?"

"I don't suppose they will, but we would have to lie in order to have you believe us and that does not sit well with me. Everything we send out comes back to us and so I am very careful about what I say. My brother in law, John Longbrooke is the Vicar at Ermington and a very holy man he is. Always telling me about right and wrong, although I have just sold him and his brother a house and land at Ermington for only 100 marks of silver, so he should shut up for a while."

"Noble sentiments Giles, I shall make notes."

"Thanks. I can also tell you that we have no knowledge of how the *Borja* left the harbour for no one saw it leave. It is an impossible thing to happen without people noticing."

"It just vanished?"

"Yes, but it has been seen further out to sea, still surrounded by the mist and still with no crew."

"Tell me, how I am supposed to explain all of this?"

"Use what I have written there. As Burgess and MP, I should be listened to. My word is good and I have come to the conclusion that the crew of the *Borja* stole the cargo, took it away and let the ship drift to its own destiny. A ship is harder to hide than a cargo. I expect they unloaded it in Cornwall where there are many creeks in which to hide. If someone there had knowledge of it, then theft and smuggling would be easy to achieve. Or, Mr Geoffrey Chaucer, I can write down the truth and see which gaol we end up in."

Chaucer rolled up the papers and tapped his mouth with them.

"I expect they are more likely to believe that the crew are thieves than you lot had a weird adventure in some ghostly green mist. Look, I will do what you say, if you allow me to use your story and write it up at some point in the future? It will make a great poem or play."

"As you please, but I don't really think of it as an adventure. Wherever we were for those hours, I had an awful feeling that we could have been stuck there and I believe that the crew and the cargo are stuck somewhere too. Whether it is in another time or place, I know not. It is not the only ship that has gone missing on this coastline with no explanation."

Hawley interrupted, "It was the strangest experience of my life and I don't want it to happen again. And the next time I see a ghost ship, I am leaving it alone."

"Fine, but buy me supper tonight," said Chaucer.

BURIAL GROUND

Featuring Sir John Prideaux (1380-1443)

Sir John Prideaux used to have a lot of problems falling asleep but now it seemed that waking up was becoming the problem.

He had been going to sleep at around midnight and then waking up a couple of hours later remembering. He had much to remember, Agincourt, Joan of Arc, both events still sickened him to the core. Recently John, his eldest son and heir had died and that meant that all the Horilake properties had gone to his daughter Joan and so to her husband Robert Stretchley. Effectively those lands were now out of John's control and the income with it. But he still had Adeston and his businesses in Totnes and Dartmouth begun by his father Giles, now long dead.

Financially this branch of the family was sound, it was the guilt and the deaths which ran around and around his mind incessantly. He had refused to take any part in the shameful slaughter of those noble French prisoners at Agincourt, but had been forced by King Henry to watch the murder – not execution as it had been sold back home. John had considered it murder and he had known some of those French noblemen. Not for them the glorious death in battle, but the slow swipe of the dagger or the badly aimed arrow. John had thought that bad enough to not be sorry when he heard of Henry's death from dysentery at the same battle field John had been on. Then having to be present with the Duke of Bedford and Sir John Robeassart, the Captain of the Castle of Saint Sauvieur le Viscount when they killed that young French girl because they had no other way to deal with her, was almost too traumatic. The screams of all of those dying souls, invaded his mind every time he tried to relax.

Sir John's coping mechanisms had become ridiculous. He had been washing his hands and body over and over, never feeling that the blood was washed away. Then he discovered that his own eyes would cloud over with flashing lights accompanied by a terrible headache, which could not be relaxed with rest or potion. He assumed he was trying to unsee all he had seen.

Now, following that evening visiting what he had been told was an ancient burial ground at the southern edge of his lands and banked on the River Erme, he had been unable to wake up without a servant shaking him vigorously. The supposed burial ground looked nothing more than a copse in a riverside meadow, grazed by cattle and ponies, although John had to admit that this was an area, covered by willow, hazel and elm trees, where no bird flew nor nested. When they hunted that spot, the horses would rear and refuse to enter and the dogs ran in any direction other than into the copse.

It was Richard Wodeland who had taken him. They dealt with each other in business and a few years ago, John had bought some land from him between Dartmouth and Torre. John was also trying to recoup land which had been taken from them by the Crown in order to save the skin of an ancestor cousin who had killed a Bigbury, but was only able to buy back field by field whenever the Bigbury's needed money.

That night, Wodeland rode with him, saying that he had known about this place since a child. Some Prideaux ancestor had told a Wodeland ancestor – Peter Prideaux had once been a ward of the Wodelands – after he had heard it from a coven which used to operate around here. Or perhaps still did, Wodeland didn't know. John Prideaux knew. His grandmother had been part of the coven and his current, living wife, was also a member. John knew about them and their practices, but had not known of the burial ground. He was eager to see it.

The horses would not go too near and so the men left them on a long tether to graze and they walked to the copse. It did look different in moonlight, but that was to be expected. A cloudless night with a full moon and a quiet river did not feel safe. Somehow a wailing wind or lashing rain was something to work against or run from. This sneaky peacefulness meant John thought of a dastardly shape hiding behind that tree, or a sea monster hiding on the bank waiting for him to pass so that it could creep behind him as he walked. John shivered and Richard looked at him,

"You alright John? I told you it was creepy here."

"You did. But I have been in such terrible places in my life and not felt as I do here, tonight."

"Come on, let's hurry into the copse. I want us to be ready for when it happens."

"When what happens?" asked John, shocked. His anxiety had been rising since they left the horses and as his level of anxiety was often too high, for no outward reason, the current shocks were almost paralysing him.

"When the spirits from the graves walk. I told you, didn't I? Or did I forget? It's a very interesting experience and one that very few have seen."

"You told me no such thing Wodeland and I wouldn't have come, had I known."

"Don't be such a baby. You have seen more than this on those battle fields."

"Perhaps, but I am not eager to see any more horrors."

"You will find it all very interesting. Come on, stop wasting time."

The resulting episode would not leave John's mind. They reached the centre of the copse, John with leaden legs until he drank a large swig of the proffered wine, and they both sat on a fallen tree, now covered in furry moss. Richard placed his finger on his lips, signalling silence and John tried to keep his mind in check. It was telling him to leave, right now before he fainted or passed out or died. However, he was used to these feelings and so did nothing.

Then they heard a whispering of men's voices, although they could not understand what was being said. They jumped from the stump and moved silently behind a large elm tree from behind which, they peeped. The men were dressed in tunics and leggings similar to that which men from 300-400 years ago had worn. These clothes must have been blue or grey in colour as the men seemed almost invisible. They carried swords, unsheathed. One spirit turned his head in the men's direction and John was horrified to see that it was nothing but a skull with hair. John gasped and Richard slapped his hand across John's mouth.

The spirit moved its head from side to side trying to locate the sound. Unable to tune in, it walked forward with its associates. A mist rose and John thought of a tale his father had told him once of a ghost ship. Giles had told him that he thought he might have travelled in time and John considered the possibility that he and Richard had too.

The spirit men looked from side to side and moved on through the trees and out of sight.

"It's not over yet!" said Richard with glee.

A line of monks passed through, heads bowed and chanting. The last monk carried a small child which whimpered and shouted for his mama. John tried to get up to rescue it, but Richard held him back.

"Phantoms," he reminded him.

Then arrived twenty, thirty men dragging other men and forcing them to kneel facing John and Richard.

"Haven't seen this lot before," muttered Richard.

"I have," said John. "Agincourt."

The spirits reinacted the scene he had watched twenty years ago, horrific, bloody and pathetically noisy. John wretched and tears welled in his eyes as the executioners re-sheathed their swords and daggers and the dead fell to the ground.

"Oh, my Lord God," gasped Richard. "That wasn't very jolly." He took another swig from the bottle.

"I never wanted to see that again. Henry was a barbarian."

When a group of men spirits arrived next, surrounding a praying and very small woman to the centre of the trees and some began raising a pole, John got up and said,

"No, no, no, no. I'm going!"

He ran to his horse, untethered it and mounted as Richard arrived puffing and wheezing.

"Do you know what they did?"

"Yes, I do. I don't know what is happening here or if it is your idea of a joke, but I'm not having it."

"It's not me John! I told you the copse is haunted!"

John kicked his horse on and did not stop galloping until he brought the sweating, panting animal to the stables at Adeston and handed over the reins to a very cross and disapproving servant.

That was last week and now when John went to bed, he fell asleep too quickly and could not be woken. He spent his days at the cemetery where his two previous wives, Isabelle Bromford and Maude French and he and Isabelle's son John, were buried. He felt guilty and responsible and apologised to them for spending so much time abroad fighting and working for the King. Then he would visit his daughters Elizabeth and Julian and their husbands', William and Adam Somaster at Old Port and Jane and her husband William Drew at their own manor. He would tell them how much he loved them and they told him that they loved him and was he feeling well?

Every evening Sir John ate scantily and then went to bed to fall unconscious, sometimes before he properly undressed. Twice Richard Wodeland took him back to the copse to see if it had all been a trick of the light and twice nothing happened. John was becoming weaker in mind and body and his wife and children were all very concerned. His heir William, began asking him about the estates and how he should best run them and John realised that he had to get a grip of himself. He must get out of this depression and anxiety that was making him a nuisance.

He became conscious that his body was being shaken and opened his eyes.

"My Lord! My Lord! You are asleep again! Wake up Sir John!"

He dreamily came around and sat up in bed. His wife Anne, bustled in and told the servant to open the shutters and windows.

"John, this has to stop! It is the middle of the day and men have been awaiting your instructions for the day's work. William has instructed them and sent them on their way. Thank God that he knows his duty!"

She went to the bed and said,

"Read this book. It was written by your ancestor Richard and offers some explanation of your life. Do not come down until it has been read."

John got up and relieved himself in the bucket behind the curtain in his room. He swilled his hands and face in the bowl of cold water previously brought in by the servant and went back to bed. He reached over to the food and drink placed on his bedside table and opened the book. He had been made to read it by his father and then tested on its contents many times. He had found it boring and forgotten most of it. He realised he had also forgotten that he must pass on its contents to his own son and felt ashamed.

He read,

You are dreaming your life and will not be free until you wake. In order to wake, you must first discover where you are sleeping.

That seemed familiar. He remembered the discussions on the actual reality of life and how we are unconsciously creating all that happens to us. Once we create consciously, we are beginning to free ourselves.

He heard,

"Wake up! Sir John wake up!" He must have fallen asleep again, how annoying.

He opened his eyes and stared disbelieving into the face of his son in law, William Somaster. Standing next to him was his brother Adam.

"Oh, thank the Lord. You are alive!"

"I don't understand," he whimpered. John felt cold and wet.

"You were washed ashore, Sir John. Were you out in a boat? We saw lights at the old copse across the river there and came to investigate."

"We thought there was a fire, the flames were so high! There is nothing there now though. Were you there, Sir John?"

John sat up and looked across to the copse and saw Richard Wodeland. The sun was rising and it was quite easy to see him. Richard waved.

"Look there!" Adam pointed across the river.

"Ah, I see. A line of soldiers, is it? Where are they going?"

"Am I awake or asleep?" asked John.

"Ill and in shock, I should say Sir. Here, let us help you onto the cart and we shall take you home where your daughters may care for you."

John shivered and shook as the fur cloak was placed around his shoulders, but he realised that his anxiety had left him. He felt confident and relaxed.

"I am awake now and I have been asleep for so long. It has all been a dream We are all dreaming this. I can't die, you can't die, no one dies, because we are already dead."

William and Adam Somaster looked at each other and pulled faces.

"I hope the old boy isn't going senile," said William.

"Such a shame," agreed Adam.

IT IS DIFFICULT TO RECOGNISE A GHOST

Featuring William Prideaux (1422-1472)

When I was first introduced to Rose, I thought I would never want another woman. It wasn't the fact that she was Cornish, itself a great bonus, it was that she was just so pretty and nice. Her mother told mine, when they met at Pridias Hall on a visit once, that their family had Pridias blood in their line and my mother agreed that we would make a good match. So that was how we ended up married – our mothers decided. We married at Treffrey would you believe, for Rose's sister Elizabeth had married into that family and they were nicely ensconced in the magnificent property overlooking the harbour. I loved watching the chain being raised at the harbour mouth when invasion or attack was feared from pirates, or worse, Bretons.

But she died trying to give birth to our son William, who also died. God had chosen to leave them both in agonies and blood-covered terror for three days. It was terrible and I could not bear to view either of them as they lay in a joint coffin. I cannot remember much of the funeral, but I have been to so many over the years.

Mother said that I must marry again and get an heir and so I married little Joan Fortescue. The Fortescues of Fallapit, Allington and our family have been friends for ever and Joan and I used to play and ride together when we were small. I know that she was upset when I married Rose, but it was out of my hands. She was happy that she had me next and I tried very hard to love her. I could only think of her as a sister and found it difficult to perform, my marital duties. However, I managed to get her pregnant quite early on and so did not have to worry about that side of things until at least after the birth.

It was another son, born alive and a huge boy! He ripped apart little Joan and she died the next day from blood loss. My boy William, died an hour after he was born and they were buried together in another oak coffin. Her parents were devastated and I saw her mother glaring at me from behind her veil as though it were my fault somehow. I could not attend the funeral, I don't attend funerals any longer. Too morbid and final.

My third wife Alice, was the daughter and heir of Stephen Gifford of Theuborough. She inherited a huge house, estates and manors, which naturally were under my control as were my own estates. It became difficult to run the two, Theuborough being north of Dartmoor, but I was ready for the challenge. I spend a lot of time travelling between my properties aswell as Dartford and Totnes and spent little time at home. We have lots and lots of money, however.

Alice knew her job and set about it immediately. John arrived within a year of our marriage, Fulke a year later and after a few mishaps, Joan appeared in 1468. I decided early on that John would have my estates south of the moor and Fulke all properties north. My wife and I played cards to decide that problem. Joan married an Acland, so that was all very tidy.

I must say that I have been quite upset lately with that dreadful William Wollacombe being at Theuborough all the time. Now, he has always been a friend of mine, we have hunted and dined on many occasions. Indeed, my wife and I were most solicitous to him when his own wife died. I just feel that he has been taking advantage of our hospitality and spending too much time at Theuborough. On many occasions, I have seen him with my dear Alice even when I am out of the house. Only yesterday I arrived back from an errand to find him eating in the dining hall with Alice as though he was Master! I went in and remonstrated with them, but both got up and left the room without speaking to me.

Another peculiar thing happened last week, I believe it was. I was walking along the beach at Bude. It was early morning and no one was about. I jumped onto the sand and as the sea was quite a way out, I thought I should take a good long walk from the estuary northwards. It was very bracing and I was glad of my cloak. I became aware of someone following me after around ten minutes. Although I couldn't possible say that he was actually following, he may have merely been walking in the same direction as me, with similar intentions. That of wasting a morning in exercise.

It is a common trait amongst men to look behind at various intervals and gauge the distance of another walker. I certainly did and noted that he was gaining on me. Only slightly, but gaining nonetheless. I walked a little quicker trying to lose him, but this man, no doubt fitter than I, was still gaining ground on me.

I don't really know why, but it made me feel uncomfortable. As he neared I swore that I could hear muttering or perhaps the squealing of a suckling pig. I did not like it and so at the earliest opportunity I left the beach via a low cliff and stood on the meadow there. Now, I intended to walk back to Bude along the cliff and not the beach. This was a shame, but I felt more comfortable doing so.

The man had stopped moving northwards and stood facing me from the beach as I stood on the clifftop. He had his hands on his hips and was staring at me. I waved and the man turned and ran, ran mark you, back southwards to Bude. I made up my mind to walk back across country to Theuborough, in case the man meant me harm.

I muttered to myself on the walk, firstly that I wished that I had ridden to Bude, but I hadn't, so there it was. Then I began to wonder if, and soon became firmly convinced that, Woolacombe was something to do with the strange man. By the time I had reached Launcells Cross and saw a man swinging from a gibbet there, I was sure. I stopped to look at the blackened corpse and fancied that I heard him say,

"You too then?"

I answered, "What do you mean?" before I realised that it was ridiculous to talk to a corpse and I scurried away.

When I walked up the driveway to Theuborough Hall, I was surprised to see another man staring at me, but not addressing me. This time it was the Rector. Now this man knows me very well and yet he says nothing to me? I chose to begin a conversation.

"Hello Rector. Is there a problem at the house? Is Alice alright?"

He nodded to me, said, "No Sir, no, there is no problem. Alice, Lady Prideaux, is fine." He clutched his Bible to his breast and ran towards the gate.

Now I was sure. There was a problem and he doesn't want to tell me. Why not? Well, he feels guilty, not upset and there was only one thing to feel guilty about. Woolacombe! I ran up the drive and saw Woolacombe climbing onto his horse and being assisted by my very own servant. I rushed towards them shouting,

"Woolacombe! What are you doing here again?"

I must have startled his horse with my shrieking, for it reared straight up and Woolacombe fell roughly to the ground. He moaned and groaned and his leg was bent in a horrible way. I felt guilty and said,

"Will, I am sorry."

He did not answer me and when my darling Alice ran out, I apologised to her for my display. She must have been very cross with me, for she pushed me out of the way and fell next to Woolacombe, crying!

For his part, Will Woolacombe pointed at me and said, "You devil you! Keep away from me! You are trying to kill me!"

Alice turned to face me and she screamed too!

"William! What are you doing? Why are you trying to kill Will!"

The servants were becoming restless and panicky and the horse ran down the drive.

"What is the matter with you all?" I shouted.

They were all crying and screaming and wailing and Woolacombe held his leg and shouted for help. The noise was so dreadful that my son Fulke came out of the house.

"Father! I don't understand!"

He was white faced and looked shocked.

"Fulke, I have only been for a walk and come back to this. Why is Will Woolacombe being treated as though he lives here?"

"Because he does Father! He and Mother married last year. After you died! You fell from you horse and broke your neck, don't you remember?"

There was still much whimpering, some of it coming from me. I ran into Theuborough Hall and up the stairs to my own rooms, where I looked out from the window. From there I heard,

"Mother, I told you I had seen Father's spirit. He doesn't seem to understand that he is dead."

"Fetch the Rector. He must bless the house again. It isn't your father, it is the Devil!"

Later that evening, Fulke came into my rooms and walked over to my chair.

"You are not visible to me now Father and ask your indulgence over this. I know you are here somewhere in this room and I know that you are not the Devil. But really, if you wish to carry on living here, you must stop scaring people and accept that you must not walk about the neighbourhood in the daylight. Be like other ghosts and stick to the night hours."

So that is what I do. I only come out at night, when people find it difficult to recognise a ghost.

THE TERROR OF THE THUNDERSTORM

Featuring John Prideaux (1461 – 1523)

John loved owning property and he loved being rich. He had inherited all the Prideaux properties in the South Hams from his father William and would also inherit the huge properties in North Devon should his brother Fulke die childless. Fulke had married Sir Richard Edgecombe's daughter Jane and she had died in childbirth. Depressed Fulke confirmed their father's wish that John and his heirs would inherit everything upon Fulke's death. However, Fulke had his libido roused by Katherine, the clever daughter of Sir Humphrey Poyntz. During the following fifteen years, Fulke and Katherine had driven home with a mallet, that John would not be inheriting any of the properties north of the moor, by producing 13 children.

However, John married Sybil Luson who was heiress of lands and manors adjacent to John's properties at Orcherton and Adeston. They were relatively happy together and produced four sons, Hugh, John, Henry and Thomas. The boys were a joy to their parents, full of life and competing with each other at every opportunity. John and Sybil would have liked to share the inheritance between the boys, but understood that to split the properties too much could result in their eventual loss. But, to give the eldest everything in this day and age, put him at risk of losing it anyway, because of the expenses.

The matter was settled by willing Orcherton and Adeston to Hugh, Woodland, Stowford and land round Ermington and the Ivy Bridge to John and the remaining lands between Henry and Thomas. The two youngest naturally had less land and a smaller share in the Dartmouth and Totnes businesses.

Their life was happy and privileged and there were no issues, except perhaps the marked increase in severe thunderstorms over the years. None of them really minded a storm, in fact it was quite exciting to watch the sky, either sea side or moor side, flashing and crashing as the storm raged. They felt sorry for the sailors or the shepherds, knowing that neither would be able to escape the hot and wet dramas. The boys would count the time lag between the flash and the bang and tease each other how long they dare stay outside.

John and Sybil remembered their experience of childhood storms. Storms had been few and far between but exciting nonetheless. This year, storms during the summer were occurring two or three times a month. The storm would announce its arrival early, with the air becoming more humid followed by a strange silence among the birds. The sky darkened and a low grumbling in the distance signalled the direction from which the storm would appear. Then the rain, often so heavy you could be drenched in seconds, was followed dramatically by thunder and lightning.

It was terrific when the storm swirled around the property and scary as it neared. If the dark also accompanied the event, then extra excitement was enjoyed or endured, depending upon your feelings.

Of course, that was the usual way a storm occurred. The pattern had however, begun to alter of late. The increasing regularity was the first thing that was noticed.

"There were three last week," said Sybil's maid, Netta.

"And the week before," agreed Sybil.

"My father told me that it was the Devil throwing burning rocks at God," Netta informed her mistress.

"I thought it was God moving his furniture around?" said Sybil.

"But why? If that was the case, then we would hear him stomping about or moving his chair from his table," said Netta reasonably.

"I have a feeling that it is really unusual weather systems," noted Sybil with finality.

A few weeks later, young Jonny came into his mother's rooms and said,

"Mama, when we had that horrible storm last night, I looked out of the window. I know I shouldn't, but I did. And I saw something very horrible in the garden by the sundial when the lightning flashed."

Sybil hugged him and asked, "What did you see Jonny?"

"I saw a very tall man and he was dressed like a monk. He had a black robe and a big hood which was pulled up against the rain, I suppose. There was a rope around his waist with something dangling from it, probably prayer beads. His head was bowed and as I was watching him, he suddenly raised his head and he could see inside his hood! It was a skull!"

"Oh dear, you must have been very scared. What happened next?"

"The next flash of lightning came and he was gone, so I suppose he went into the trees. I hope he didn't get into the Hall, because he didn't look very nice."

"Perhaps it was the lightning that made a small tree or a statue look like a monk. There are plenty there," pointed out Sybil.

"I knew you would say that Mama, so I made sure. It was a monk and he was horrible."

Sybil kissed him and sent him on his way, but when she told John later, she said,

"Jonny doesn't lie, nor does he make mistakes. Make sure the servants keep a look out. Some of these monks are not so nice."

"No, but he may have been a hermit, they are often seen after travelling from Ireland or Wales to Cornwall."

"I know and I don't mind that. I don't mind when you provide them with food and shelter, I know how much all this magical nonsense means to your family, but I don't want to be murdered in my bed by a crazy foreigner pretending to be a holy man."

"Nonsense? It's not nonsense, but I have to admit that the stories are being forgotten. I keep losing that old book of Richard de Pridias. I go and look for it in the library, just to check and I can't find it and then another time, I can. I wonder if…"

"John, don't ramble. Make sure there are no intruders, will you?"

John huffed out of the room and went downstairs. He instructed Philip to post a man at the door each night as there had been sightings of a strange man outside.

"Is it the monk?"

John stopped.

"Yes, have you seen him?"

"No Sir. Quite a few people have though. They say he comes with the storms and is a sign of danger."

"I doubt that. Let's make sure he cannot get into the house. If the man is in need, feed him, give him a few coins and send him on his way. My wife and children are becoming alarmed."

"Yes Sir."

The following week, there was a heavy storm every day. Even though it was now midsummer, the days never really got properly light. As soon as the sun came out, the air became leaden and humid. The women fanned themselves and wore fewer clothes under their tunics and found excuses to splash themselves with water. Many were breathless with heat, which by midday was almost unbearable and some people had died as a result. By around mid-afternoon, the rain came and then the black and dreadful storm.

Cattle and sheep were getting hit by the lightning and killed. People, instead of joking and keeping away from trees and open spaces, fearfully ran for their houses and barns as the jagged lightning cracked across the sky. After the storms, which would often carry on rumbling through the evening and night, jobs were caught up on and visits done quickly.

On one of these days, Sybil shouted to John as he returned from an early morning trip to another part of the estate.

"John! Jonny is missing! He went to look for his dog and I don't know where he is. I don't want him hurt!"

John remounted and he and his servant rode towards the coast, in the direction pointed out by his wife. The clouds were thickening and both men were conscious that the storm could not be far away. The horses were not as forward going as they had been and John needed to squeeze encouragement to his mount. Cottagers and workmen raised their arms or hats, depending on their sex, then went for shelter remarking how stupid John Prideaux was to be out in this weather.

The rain began to fall and they pulled their cloaks tighter. They had to slow to a walk by the time they arrived at Mothecombe, for the incoming tide was raising the river levels quite high and they didn't want to slip. The thunder had begun now and looking out to sea, they saw ships, over and under whelming as they tried to gain control. John had never liked the sea and was glad that he had never been forced to travel abroad by an Earl or King.

"Jonny! Jonny!" they shouted and received no answer.

The lightning had come and it cracked on the horizon. As the shore lit up, John saw what he thought was a cloaked man standing a distance away from them. A minute more and another flash, nearer this time and he thought the man was nearer also, although he hadn't seen him move.

"Sir, we should find shelter."

"Yes, but my son may not be in shelter and I can't bear that. We must find him." This plea could not be ignored by Philip and he pushed his horse forward towards the man.

"I say! You! Have you seen a boy? A ten-year-old boy?"

There was no answer and another flash of lightning lit up the scene. The cloaked man was now within throwing distance, although nothing was thrown.

"Perhaps he doesn't understand. Perhaps he only speaks Gaelic?" said John.

"He shouldn't be here then," answered Philip. "What is beginning to bother me Sir, is that lightning is coming in a direct line towards us. If it does not divert, one of those flashes is going to hit us."

John shouted to the man.

"We are looking for my son. He is possibly with a small dog. Please, have you seen him?"

The monk walked towards the men and another lightning strike hit the coastline. He held out his hands towards a tree just in front of John and Philip. The next strike they didn't see, just heard. An echoing crack and blackness all around.

"We are dead," John said out loud.

"I think we are Sir," answered Philip.

The monk stood in front of them and handed them a parchment.

"A prayer, John Prideaux. Read it, repeat it and make sure your family uses it always. It works particularly well in times of strife. Such as when your boy and his dog are missing in a thunderstorm. It was sent by the Disperkel."

He bowed and vanished into the blackness.

"Should I read it now, do you think?" asked John.

"Yes Sir."

John read,

O God, That knowest us to bee set in the midst of so many and great dangers, that for Mans frailenesse we cannot always stand uprightly, guard to us the health of Body and Soul, that all those things which we suffer for sinne, by thy holy wee may well passe and overcome, through Jesus Christ our Lord.

It was light and the storm had passed. The ground on all sides of the two men was blackened and burnt and there was a dreadful smell of singeing. The ships were settled on the sea and birds had begun their songs.

"Papa! Papa!"

Running towards them was Jonny and his dog.

"I was lost Papa! I went to a strange place full of people who said they knew me. And there were wolves! But everything is alright now. Can we go home?"

John pulled his son up onto his horse and they rode slowly back home, the dog trotting behind.

"What is the Disperkel?" asked Philip.

"He is something to do with our lands in Cornwall. From hundreds of years ago."

John resolved to find that old book when he got home and keep it properly safe.

That was the last storm of the season, but not the last time the monk was seen by a Prideaux.

www.ingramcontent.com/pod-product-compliance
Lightning Source LLC
Chambersburg PA
CBHW050320200626
46812CB00019BA/2852